A Stitch In Time

A novella
Written by S. G. Lee

SB

An imprint of Shillelagh Books
London, Ontario, Canada

Acknowledgments:
Sincere thanks to Jodi and Sydney, without your constant support and encouragement, this book would not be possible. You are the best friends a writer could have. I dedicate this book to my daughters, my son-in law and my husband; who have supported my writing endeavours with encouragement and love. Special thanks to my beloved mother in heaven, who taught me dreams, can come true with hard work, perseverance and patience.

Table of Contents

Preface: A note from the writer

This is a novella about Emmett Rogers, the soon to be policeman who is in the Kelly Murder Mysteries. This is his back story before the Kelly Murder Mysteries. Please read on....

Chapter 1 - Home Sweet Home

Emmett Rogers adjusted his bag on his shoulder, as he got out of the cab. Emmett breathed a sigh of relief; he was home, back in Canada, Happy Valley, Ontario to be exact. His experiences had taken him a world away both in distance and in emotions. The squad had been his family, but that was over. They had been severed because of their experiences.

He'd missed his hometown and his crazy mixed up family as well. When 911 had occurred he like many other Canadians were at first shocked, then horrified, then angry that someone would harm their dearest neighbour who they considered family. And what do you do when someone harms family and continues to threaten a family member? You fight back and that is what Emmett had done. He had left university in London, Ontario and enlisted. They called it peacekeeping, but he fought terrorists in Afghanistan.

Two days before he left, Jenna, his long term girlfriend, told him she was pregnant. Emmett had been horrified at first after all he was shipping out. He wasn't ready to be father and a soldier. Jenna told him she was sorry it was all her fault. She had forgotten to take her birth control pill just once but once was enough. Then she started crying and before he knew it Emmett was proposing. They quietly wed at the courthouse downtown. Jenna then moved in with his folks.

Emmett went off to the war and was sent on a secret mission that he still couldn't talk about with the Americans in October of 2001. Then in January and February of 2002 he and three other Princess Patricia's Canadian Light Infantry snipers fought a long side the Americans during Operation Anaconda. The team broke, and re-broke, the kill record for a long distance sniper kill set in the Vietnam War by a U.S. Marine which made Emmett and his team really happy but it was when they started to think about the kills that Emmett became troubled. This haunted him in his dreams at night and when he received a letter that hadn't reached him in early January. Jenna told him the sad news that their baby had been born stillborn a beautiful baby girl; too tiny to survive.

His nightmares got worse. In his dreams he tried to save Jenna but in doing so he killed their unborn child. Emmett wondered if all the killing he'd done had truly killed his child karma reaching out to pay him back. He became despondent and distracted. The other soldiers were worried about being with him and they spoke to their superiors. Emmett pulled himself together but he was transferred to Kandahar where they gave him different duties; one of them trying to teach the Afghans how to fight the Taliban. Emmett then learned that being a soldier wasn't exactly what he thought. Some of his work was strictly peacekeeping, other times it was the fight against insurgents. None of this was what he expected but it was his job and he protected people; he chose this career he'd tough it out then get home to Jenna. Jenna had endured worse' she'd been alone even with his parents losing their child. He had to serve his term and get back to her.

Jenna waited for him living with his parents. He was so lucky that she hadn't given up on him this last four years, while he was overseas. She could have done so. Some of his buddies had gotten 'Dear John letters'. He admired her for sticking out living with his dad as he knew he could be old fashioned and difficult to live with.

Emmett had done a lot of soul searching when it came to re-enlisting, but he knew he had to get out of Afghanistan before it he was killed like so many of his fellow soldiers. Hell he'd survived so many incidents in which he should have been killed that his fellow officers called him 'The Cat'. At first he too had laughed about that. It was either laugh, or admit he could die, but after surviving friendly fire; he knew he too could die. He had continued to have nightmares different ones and days when he would sweat and slip back to the scene with soldiers all around him either injured or dying. He had tried to block it out so much that he became aloof and seemed uncaring. They had reassigned him to Kabul to train civilians in digging wells and repairing buildings, his other job... training, civilians to take over as police officers.

They hoped that this would make it possible for police to keep the peace and keep the terrorists at bay and they could protect themselves. Often though, he and other Canadian soldiers had trained men to be Afghan policemen and those they trained were sometimes turning on the very soldiers who taught them, planting roadside bombs for the patrols to die in, or just shooting them. Or those good men, who trained to become police officers, would be killed, for working with the Canadians. It became harder to tell who the enemy were and who the innocents were. Especially when young teens would ambush the soldiers and it was kill or be killed.

Emmett had felt if he stayed much longer he might lose his humanity. He'd also started having more, and more, nightmares, and cold sweats, about all that he had done in the battles. Emmett told he suffered from post-traumatic stress disorder, sought help for it. His psychiatrist said he blamed himself for the deaths of fellow soldiers and for the insurgents, he killed. With treatment he felt better.

Coming home it felt like he had lost the last four years, he felt younger, cleaner, and not as tarnished yet he knew that was an illusion. He had survived four year of combat, but he had changed; he couldn't deny that. Maybe the simple act of being home would change him back. Make him whole again. He hoped so.

He looked forward to seeing how much his little sisters had grown. Paula, was seventeen now and Suzy, was fifteen, almost sixteen years old. His sisters were young women. How had that happened?

Letters from Suzy had been cheerful but if he read behind the lines he knew she struggled with their father and his alcoholism. Dad had been a drinker as long as Emmett could remember. He'd taken the belt and his fists to Emmett but Suzy was his favourite, he wouldn't have abused her. Would he have? It would be fine now; Emmett would be home to protect her and Paula. His father wouldn't harm any of them.

Emmett saw the sun rise over his parent's house and he smiled. Five a.m. and he was ecstatic. It felt good to be home. The sun started to filter its rays opening up his view of the town below his parent's home. The Canadian Shield nestled high about twenty feet above his parent's backyard also told him he was home. The rock face had that distinctive look that he knew so well. He was home his heart sang. Home!!!

He had a week's leave and then he start with the Happy Valley police department next week. He would make a good police constable and his captain had put a good word in for him, getting him a start as a third class constable. He stuck his key in the door and turned it only to have the door yanked open by his mother, Matilda nestled in her arms, the cat, Nicodemus.

Nicodemus turned up his nose at Emmett, hissed and then stalked off when he tried to pet him.

"Emmett? Is it really you? Oh thank God, you're an answer to my prayers. He's gone absolutely mad, and I can't find her."

"Who is mad, mom? And who can't you find?"

"Your father has thrown out Paula, just like he did my Dianna."

Emmett wasn't surprised. His father was an egomaniac. It was his way or the highway. Emmett was scared that he wouldn't find Paula; but he tried not to show it. He started to sweat and almost fell to his knees, but composing himself he closed his eyes and counted to thirty, as his psychiatrist had taught him. He wouldn't fall apart, he had to help Paula. Dianna had left home and disappeared; that couldn't happen to Paula. He wouldn't allow it. He was a man now; he could change this.

Thirteen years... had it really been thirteen years that Dianna had been missing? He missed her everyday but somehow in some ways it seemed like yesterday.
Father had argued with Dianna. Dianna had wanted to go to a school dance a simple school dance. Mom had said yes, of course she could go. Dianna had bought a new dress and red one that hung just above her knees. She earned the money babysitting and she was happy oh so happy. It sparkled and swung in a circle when she moved and gleeful showed to their mother. That's when dad came home drunk as a skunk. How he had time enough to drink that much before seven p.m. Emmett didn't know.

Emmett had been playing with his *Grayskull* castle and his *He-Man*; his father kicked the castle and swore as he tripped. He then spotted Dianna twirling in her dress. Father then called her a whore. He claimed the dress was indecent and that no daughter of his would go out in that especially not to a dance. She argued back and he struck her. Emmett tried to stop him, but he was only a small boy pulling at the arms and legs of a grown man. His father beat both Dianna and Emmett merciless. Finally he stopped drank a beer and passed out.

Emmett's mother tended Emmett's wounds and put him to bed and then tended Dianna wounds. When Emmett woke up the next morning Dianna was gone. Emmett's mother told her children not to tell the police about the fight and to keep silent and for her they had. But maybe it was time to tell the police what happened all those years ago. Had Dianna really left or had his father killed her?

No, Dianna had left of her own volition. Her things were packed up by her and yet doubts remained in his mind. His father could have disposed of her things or someone else could have taken her...killed her.

Police had come and gone, reports had been made, but Dianna hadn't been found. He had since learned a serial killer had been operating in the area around that time. He had to face the facts, she was probably dead; though he searched and searched since his teen years no trace of Dianna had ever been found. He didn't want this to happen to Paula... it couldn't. He still had nightmares where he couldn't find Dianna. Maybe it was time to get his mother and his sisters safely away. He was stronger now a man.

"Tell me what happened this time, mother."

"Don't you speak to your mother that way you ingrate. I can tell you what happened, son. That little kitten in heat, found some tom cat to service her, and now she's up the stump, so I threw the whore out," answered his father.

"How dare you call my sister, a whore!" Emmett shouted.

"I'll say anything I want. She was under my roof!" Tobias Rogers shouted back.

"But she's not under your roof, now is she? And where is Dianna? We haven't seen her in thirteen years"

"Don't back talk back to me, boy and don't you mention her name in my house. That little bitch; did she think of her mother or father? No, she just took off and never spoke to us again," his father answered.

"Maybe because you mistreated her," Emmett retorted.

"Think you're bigger and stronger than me because you've been in the army? I'll take you down a peg or two!"

Tobias then put his hand out to strike Emmett. Emmett looked at him and his mind an insurgent came at him and he grabbed the man's arm and put him in a choke hold protecting his family.

"Emmett, please, you're hurting your father. Emmett stop it, now," Matilda (his mother) cried.

"Emmett, do you hear me? Let go of Dad. It's okay Emmett. I know he provoked you," Suzy cried, sizing up the situation as she came into the kitchen.

Emmett realized what he had been doing and he let go of his father. He felt ashamed how could he have thought he was in Afghanistan? That his father was an insurgent? He was a silly old man, with no real strength; not like in the past. The man couldn't harm anyone. Emmett was safe and so was his mother and sisters. It had to be jetlag, he wasn't relapsing. He was better now he was home. This wouldn't happen again. Suzy looked at him now like he was a monster.

"I'm glad you're home Emmett. Are you okay now?" Suzy asked concerned staring deep into his eyes.

"I'm fine, Sprite. Sorry, I lost my temper. How are you?"

"I'm not five years old anymore, Emmett. How are you really?" Suzy cried.

"I can see that," Emmett answered, "You're almost all grown-up."

"Where's my apology, boy? You could have killed me using those army techniques on me. What's wrong with you?"

Emmett's mother looked at him begging him to smooth things over and Emmett felt ashamed knowing that she had to live with this man the last four years and all the years before that. He'd make it up to her somehow but for now he'd make peace.

"Sorry, father," Emmett said just trying to keep you from hitting me."

"A slap or two is good for a child. Spare the rod and spoil the child. Says so in the bible does it, Matilda?"

"Don't you ever listen to yourself, old man? You've lost two daughters, because of your mental and physical abuse of them. Show some common sense, then perhaps we can get this child back before any more damage is done," Emmett answered.

"When you're a father boy come back and talk to me. I've got every right to discipline the girl; she's not even eighteen years old yet. Even if you find her she's not coming back here. She's disgraced the family. Let her see how hard it is too support a child."

"Disgraced the family? Then she is pregnant with your grandchild! Who throws a pregnant daughter out of the house?" Emmett yelled.

"I will hear no more of this disrespect!" Tobias shouted, "If you bring her back here you and your wife move out today. I've kept her for you boy, while you did your gallivanting playing soldier instead of taking care of your responsibilities. I put the roof over your wife and put food on her table not you!! I don't want a no-account, abusive son living with me anyway. You probably brought back one of them foreign diseases from them weird peoples."

"Fine, Jenna and I were moving out, anyway. As for Paula, if she wants, she can live with us, Jenna and me."

"Please Emmett. Don't do this. Don't move out," mother begged.

"Well that's gratitude for you. I don't care what you do, sonny boy. As of today, I have no son named Emmett, or a daughter named Paula. You think you are the only educated ones. Think on this Emmett, that Shakespeare guy was right. How sharper than a serpent's tooth to have a thankless child. You are all ungrateful little heathens, you Paula and the sainted Dianna. She was pregnant too, when I threw her out. You didn't know that while you blamed me all these years. She weren't no saint."

Matilda, Emmett's mother looked long and hard at Tobias, like she had never seen him before. Emmett knew then she had known nothing about Dianna's pregnancy; this was all a revelation to her. Maybe it wasn't even true. His father could have manufactured this excuse to shift the blame (at least in his mind) Emmett knew how much his mother grieved for Dianna. They all still did wondering if she was okay or even alive. He had thought his father had hid his grief, but it seemed that Tobias had been the one to chase Dianna away. At that moment Emmett hated him, more than he had ever hated him before.

"I'm going back to bed; don't wake me with your shouting. Take your meagre belongings and leave. Coming, Matilda?" Tobias uttered, like he was bored.

"No, I'm staying," Matilda answered defiantly, earning her a look from her husband of hatred.

"As you wish then, cater to the brats. You always do. See where that gets you. But Paula and the boy never comes back here again," Tobias yelled over his shoulder as he went back to bed.

"Don't I get consulted about Paula staying with us, Emmett?" Jenna whined.

"My sister needs me, Jenna," Emmett answered.

"Where was that concern when I needed you? Fine, do what you want. You always do," Jenna replied.

"Jenna...please, not now!"

"Do we even have somewhere to go?" Jenna asked, sounding like she conceded.

"I'll get us a place but; for now go to your friend Janie's place."

"You're assuming we're still friends."

"Aren't you?"

"Yes. Fine, I'll call pack my stuff and go there."

 I'll pick you up later, Jenna. I'm going to look for Paula. Who are Paula's friends, mom?"

"Ashley and Georgina, but she's probably with him...that awful Jason Spriet. He lives on Becker Street," Suzy answered.

"So you think Paula's at this Jason's, Suzy? What number on Becker Street?"

"Six-fifty-three, Becker."

"Okay, I'm going to find Paula."

"I'm coming with you," Suzy cried.

Matilda sighed and hugged Emmett, "I'm so glad you're home. I knew I could count on you."

"Don't worry mom, we won't let Paula disappear like Di. Come on Suzy."

Emmett ushered Suzy out the door. He'd find Paula with Suzy's help. Suzy would be safer with Emmett anyway he didn't trust his father anymore.

~0~

Chapter 2 - Jason

E mmett and Suzy reached the door of the house on

Becker Street. The screen door hung precariously from the frame. The windows of the house were covered in years of grime and the house's roof looked barely there. The backyard was filled with old decrepit cars and trucks that would never run again and a mound of other scrap metal. Someone lived here? Emmett thought he'd seen better looking shacks in Afghanistan.

"We'll find her won't we, Emmett?" asked Suzy looking scared.

"I'm going to find her, Suzy, with your help," Emmett replied.

Suzy smiled in relief and waited patiently for Emmett to knock on the door. He did so and a few minutes later the door was opened by a woman who appeared to be sixty years old. Her face was lined with wrinkles around her eyes and her bright red lipsticked mouth. The lipstick had bled into the cracks of her lips. Her hair was long gray and swept back in a ponytail. Her hands held a cigarette were stained yellow from nicotine. Her clothing was for a young woman of sixteen, experimenting with clothing styles; not an older woman as she was dressed in a tube top and tight pencil leg jeans. Emmett didn't know quite where to look; but he kept his eyes at hers.

"Do you people know what time it is? If I didn't know you, Suzy Rogers; I wouldn't even have opened the door. Now who is this with you and what do you want?"

"Hello, Ms. Spriet, is Jason here?" Suzy asked.

"He's sleeping. I think he got in at three a.m., if you think I'm waking him up..."

"I just want to ask him about Paula."

"Suzy, you do know he and Paula broke up about six or seven months ago. She accused my boy of whole lot of terrible things. She gave him a terrible time about his smoking a little Mary Jane. He was in pain and I couldn't make any brownies for him, so he smoked a little weed. Big deal! Then she tried to convince me he had tried harder drugs. Like my boy would do the hard stuff!! I don't think he wants to talk about your sister or see her, after that kind of outrageous behaviour."

"Are you sure I can't speak with him? It's really important," Suzy insisted.

"No!" she replied trying to shut the door, but Emmett put out his foot stopping it.

"Who are you to do that? I asked you before who you were but you didn't answer. I have half a mind to call the police," Ms. Spriet said, belligerently.

"I'm sorry, Mrs. Spriet, I thought it better for my sister to speak to you since you knew her. My name is Emmett Rogers."

"Oh, are you the one of the soldier boys that was in Afghanistan? I heard you went there from your mama. It's a wonderful thing you boys and girls did there; making sure them girls get to go to school, and have them freedoms same as us."

"Thank you; I appreciate your kind thoughts. We're trying to find Paula. That's why Suzy asked for your son."

"Paula had a fight with our dad and she's taken off," Suzy explained.

"Silly girl. Probably doesn't realize how good she has it at home. Course she's a lot younger than my Jason."

"How old is Jason?" asked Emmett.

"How old are you Emmett?"

"Twenty-two."

"Jason's a year older then you he's twenty-three, and he'll be twenty-four in two months. Of course, sometimes he acts like a teenager. Boys will be boys," his mother excused.

Emmett was appalled. Paula was only seventeen years old and Jason had been dating her! Maybe he had more of his father in him, then he thought. Right now he felt like kicking the shit out of the little worm. Dating an underage girl and then dropping her. What kind of man does that? Oh, no poor Paula. Was she six months pregnant, and not only dad kicked her out, but Jason dropped her as well.

"Can we please speak with Jason? We have to find my sister, Mrs. Spriet."

"It's not Mrs. Thank you kindly, though. See I was never married, handsome. You can call me Ms., or Tara," she said smiling and flirting outrageously with Emmett.

"Your son, Jason, Ms. .Spriet...can we speak with your son?"

"Fine, but you won't be the only one to have to put up with his nastiness at being waken up at this hour."

"Thank you," Emmett answered softly.

Ms. Spriet then went into the house. Emerging a short time later she looked first perplexed then angry.

"He's not here. That damn boy came home and then left," she uttered.

Emmett tried hard to rein in his temper. It wasn't her fault Jason had scampered. He couldn't lose control again. He had to restrain himself if he hoped to find out any information; besides he wouldn't be like his old man and strike out at women. If he ever did that he might as well kill himself. He vowed when he was six years old never to be like his father.

"Do you have any idea where Jason could be?"

"He might be at her house again."

"Her house?" Suzy asked.

"Nancy Graham's apartment. He thinks I don't know he sneaks over there. She thinks she has my boy wrapped around her finger. Harrumph that girl is a piece of trash. She's just waiting around to trade up with the first man with money to come her way. She doesn't respect anyone let alone his mother. Sorry I should watch my mouth around you, Suzy. Sometimes I forget you're so young because you are so sensible."

"That's okay, Ms. Spriet, I am young. Do you have an address for Nancy?" Suzy mollified.

"Yes, just a minute it's in my address book somewhere. Just a minute,"

Ms. Spriet stepped away from the door returning with an address book still looking for the address.

"You know, maybe he shouldn't have broken up with Paula. Even with Paula's wild accusations she always treated me well, must be to do with her upbringing. Your mama, Matilda has always treated everyone like they were special and worthwhile. She never looked down her nose at me like some people," Ms. Spriet commented while searching. "Here it is 563 Wellington Street."

"And the apartment number?" Emmett asked.

"Number nine-oh-two," she answered.

"Thank you for your time, Ms. Spriet." Emmett commented.

"Nice boy that," Ms. Spriet muttered as she entered the house.

Emmett took out his phone to call a cab, but then saw one coming down the street. Flagging the cab he was rewarded with its backing up. Emmett and Suzy got in and Emmett gave the cab the address. Arriving at the address and disembarking they entered the rundown apartment building. The hallways dim and dirty seemed endless as they searched for the elevator. The place was absolute squalor, Emmett thought as he saw belongings tossed in some corners. Emmett expected to see cockroaches and other bugs scurrying out of the walls.

Entering the elevator Emmett and Suzy both hoped that it wouldn't breakdown with them in it as it quivered and made groaning noises. Finally it came to a stop not level with the floor and they hopped up to disembark. Emmett thought they better take the stairs when they were through. Suzy walked down the hall with Emmett following her and knocked on the door with a faint number nine-oh-one on it.

A bulked up man, standing about six feet, his hair short and spiky, a dirty blonde colour answered the door. Barefoot and bare chested and wearing a pair of blue checked pajama pants; the man's arms were muscular and his belly showed what is known as a six pack. Emmett thought he was just too muscular. He seen guys like that in the service and it wasn't natural. The man probably had bulked up with steroids.

A woman snuck up behind him clinging to him, her arms around his neck from behind him. Her long fingernails brushed over his chest possessively. Emmett noted her long blonde hair hung down to her waist and she was dressed only in a white tank top and a thong, but she didn't attempt to hide. The man turned to her and said, "Quit showing off your assets babe. Go put some clothes on, Nance."

Nancy then turned and went down the hall to the bedroom.

"My mom called me to tell me, Suzy was looking for me. You're not, Suzy. Who are you and what do you want? If you think a guy like you can hit on a sixteen-year-old girl on my watch, you can think again," Jason exclaimed, looking like he was ready for a fight.

"I'm Emmett Rogers, Suzy's brother."

"Emmett? No way dude, Emmett's in Afghanistan."

"This is Emmett," Suzy said.

"I'm looking for Paula, my sister," Emmett continued.

"So what do I care? Paula, I broke up with me months ago, and I have no idea where she is."

"Yah, he dumped her. She's a stupid bitch," Nancy chimed in sneaking up behind him.

Nancy was now dressed in tight jeans and the same tank top, Emmett noticed.

"Is it your baby she's pregnant with?" Suzy asked.

"Paula's pregnant? But you told me you broke up with her.
You bastard!" the woman cried hitting Jason's back with
her fists.

"I didn't make you any promises. I love Paula, but she
dumped me," Jason responded.

"That's not what you told me, or even what you said a few
minutes ago. You said you loved me," Nancy whined.

"So I lied. A man has needs, but Paula, now she's a woman
in a million."

"I'll show you a woman in a million, you bastard."

Nancy then turned on her heel and went into the back of the
apartment returning with Jason's clothes which she threw
out the window and into the street. She then pushed Jason
and some other clothes and shoes out the front door and
locked it right in front of Emmett and Suzy who were still
standing in the hallway. Emmett was surprised to see Jason
looking amused. Jason then started putting on his shirt,
socks and shoes and then his coat that he had snagged in the
hallway.

"So, Paula is pregnant Suze?"

"Yes, she told my dad yesterday and he went ballistic. He
threw her out," Suzy answered.

"Your old man is an asshole. She showed me the bruises he
gave her when she dated me."

"Son of a bitch, my dad bruised Paula?" Emmett demanded to know.

"Hell, yes! Paula said you used to keep her dad from hurting her when she was younger, by taking the beatings yourself. Did you think he stop, just because you were in Afghanistan?" Jason asked.

"But he promised he would harm them again, before I left."

"And you believed him soldier boy? Paula said you were naive and a real Dudley-Do-Right. She was right!"

Emmett felt all kinds of a fool he wasn't there for his sisters, because he had been protecting other young girls in Afghanistan, but what about his own sisters? And why did it continue to feel like he wanted to smash Jason's face? He couldn't become the man his father was.

"Did Dad hurt you, Suzy?" Emmett asked.

"No, I'm the peacemaker. I always do exactly what is expected of me and then Dad leaves me alone. But Paula antagonized him. Poor Paula, in some ways she's like Dad in personality."

"Nice family reunion you've got going on there, Rogers, but what about Paula? Do you have an idea where she is Suzy?" Jason enquired interrupting.

"I don't know. Can you think of someone she'd go to?" Suzy answered.

"That must have been why she broke up with me. I'm a fool," Jason exclaimed. "I knew she loved me. I'll make her proud of me and win her back."

"How were you going to do that Jason?" asked Suzy, "You were sleeping with another woman!"

"A man has his needs. Paula will understand. I signed up. I go for basic training tomorrow and then they're shipping me out to Afghanistan, in six weeks."

Emmett looked at Jason up and down and then retorted, "You better get in the shape of your life, because the way you look right now you won't survive two days there. It takes more than muscle mass to survive. As for Paula, you should stay the hell away from my sister."

"I already cut my hair and you can see I've got tons of muscle working for me. Ha, those insurgents better watch out for me!" Jason boasted, "As for Paula, no one is keeps me away from the mother of my child. Now let's go find my girl, I think I know where to find her."

Emmett felt queasy, he hated this man, but he didn't wish the hells of Afghanistan on anyone. Looking at him he saw Tommy. Tommy had been just like Jason, cocky, brash and extremely rash. That had gotten Tommy killed. In fact he had endangered his whole squad. Emmett worried about the troops that would serve with Jason and hoped they would not suffer the same fate as some others in Emmett's squad. Jason knew where Suzy was so he'd use him to find Paula, but he wasn't letting Paula anywhere near this jerk again.

"Emmett, are you sure you're okay? You don't look so good." Suzy asked looking at him with concern.

"I'm fine, and I'll be even better, once we find Paula."

Emmett then followed Jason as he went towards the curb.

"Well, jump in this is my ride," Jason cried opening his car.

The car's backseat was full of take-out containers, bags and old pop containers as well as a bong. Emmett considered the implications of the car being stopped and himself being arrested along with Suzy but then dismissed it. They had to find Paula even if it meant getting in this hunk of junk. Suzy and Emmett pushed some of the garbage on the floor as they climbed in the backseat. Suzy grimaced and held her nose as she caught a whiff of Jason's ripeness.

"Where do you think my sister is Jason?"

"I think Paula may be at Frannie's. She talked a lot to Frannie. That damn, Frannie! Frannie told her I smoked pot."

"Weren't you?" Suzy asked boldly.

"Yes, but that hose beast should have interfered. I won't smoke now that I've got a kid. Paula and I would have resolved that bump in the road. After all it was caused by a bump Ha, ha!"

Jason looked to see if they found that funny and seeing that they didn't he sniped "Get your seatbelts on I'm not paying the fine."

They both checked their already done up seatbelts adjusting them. Suzy managed to lacerate her finger and Emmett asked her if she had a Band-Aid.

"What do you need a Band-Aid, wuss? Oh, it's for Suzy. Here I'll get you one from the dash, Suzy-cute. Paula used to keep some there," Jason said taking his eyes off the road to open the dash.

The car swerved and Jason barely got his eyes up to look and avert an accident.

"Suzy has a small cut and she appreciates the Band-Aid Jason, please keep your eyes on the road as you pass it to her hand."

"Some people try to do them a favour and they decide they're the best drivers in the world. Just because you got to drive them tanks in Afghanistan doesn't make you a better driver. I'm going to be driving them soon, too. It doesn't make you better then me."

"Sorry, Jason I'm not trying to offend you I just want to find Paula," Emmett exclaimed trying to mollify Jason.

"So, I'm I. And because you are Paula's family, I'm putting up with you. I know you don't like me, but Paula will have my baby so you'd better get used to me dude. I'll be family, and don't you worry I'll take good care of my girl and my kid."

Emmett gave a non-committal nod and then ignoring Jason pulled out his cell phone and dialed a number.

"Paul, this is Emmett. Yes, I'm back. Things aren't working out at my folks. Do you have room in your basement for a month or so for my wife, me, and my sister? Thanks buddy, I knew I could count on you."

"Smart move, dude. Your old man's a head case. "Jason exclaimed, "I told Paula she could move in with me and get away from that old abusive prick father of hers or should I say yours?"

Emmett ignored him and hung up the cell phone smiling. He had a place to live for them. Suzy would be okay wouldn't she? Dad wouldn't touch her? Not if he told the old man he beat the crap out of him if he ever laid his hands on his daughters again. His dad didn't hurt his mom did he? He would have to find out and if necessary he'd get his mom to leave his dad and take both Suzy and Mom away too. Emmett looked up from his thoughts as they arrived at a three-storey walk-up apartment.

"Maybe you should stay here while I speak with Frannie." Jason cautioned.

Emmett's face grew angry at Jason's suggestion and he had to start counting to prevent a violent impulse to hit Jason again. What in the hell was wrong with him? He didn't lose his temper, Emmett thought. Well okay, he sometimes lost his temper, but very rarely. His motto, let things roll off his back. So why didn't that working anymore?

"Not a chance Jason. Frannie hates you she won't tell you where Paula is. Why don't you just let us talk to Frannie? Then when we find Paula we can let you know. I promise," Suzy insisted crossing her fingers behind her back where only Emmett could see.

"I guess that makes sense, but can I trust your brother not to talk smack about me?"

"He won't. Will you Emmett?"

"No, I won't," lied Emmett.

"Go then, I'll wait here. Its apartment three-hundred and two," Jason answered.

Emmett and Suzy climbed the three flights of stairs to the apartment. Emmett knocked loudly on the door.

"Who is there?" a voice asked, through the door.

"Suzy and Emmett Rogers."

The door opened a crack and a woman about twenty years old opened the door. She was skinny to the point where you could see the bones beneath her thin layer of skin at her neck. She wore a red tank top with blue jeans. A cigarette dangled from her mouth.

"Is Paula here?" asked Suzy.

"Yes, but I'm not sure she'll see you. She's upset since your daddy threw her out. I said she could chill her for a few days, but she needs to find her own place. I told her to apply for welfare. I'm not running a charity here."

"Please could you ask her if she'll speak to us?" Emmett asked.

"You're the brother that went to Afghanistan? Maybe you can straighten her out. I told her to have an abortion, months ago. Now it's too late and she keeps talking about going back to that no account, Jason Spriet. Have a seat here in the living room. I'll get her to talk to you."

"Thank you."

"Don't thank me just try to talk her out of being with that scum, Jason Spriet. He tried to pick me up behind her back. He has no morals."

A young woman with long blonde hair to her waist, walked in with great dignity, her head raised high; skinny all over, except for a bulging stomach, which looked like a beach ball under her shirt. Emmett worried that she didn't seem to have gained any weight with this pregnancy. Did she eat right? He'd have to see that she had plenty of the right kind of foods when she came to live with Jenna and him. Paula smiled at Suzy when she saw her and then gasped holding her hand to her mouth when she spotted Emmett.

"Emmett? It's really you? You're alive and okay? Oh, Emmett. It's so good to see you!" Paula cried tears streaming down her face as Emmett hugged her.

"Are you okay Paula?" Emmett asked.

"I am now that you are here. I don't know what to do Emmett. Daddy threw me out, just like he did Dianna. Just so you know, I'm pregnant and I'm keeping my baby," Paula confessed looking frightened.

"Paula it's okay, I know you are pregnant. Don't worry you and your baby can come live with me and Jenna. We're moving out of mom and dad's anyway. I'll help you anyway I can."

"Jenna? You're still with her?"

"Why wouldn't I be?"

"Paula..."Suzy started as if to shut-up her sister.

"No, Suzy he needs to know. Jenna cheated on you when you were in Afghanistan. She went out with some guys."

"You have to be mistaken I'm sure she was just out with friends."

"No, she kissed some guy when I saw her."

"Jenna was lonely. It's my fault. I wasn't there when she lost the baby, of course she'd look for comfort," Emmett responded not quite understanding why he was defended Jenna.

"You bitch, I didn't tell you Jason cheated on you, but you just had to tell Emmett," Suzy replied then covered her mouth when she realized what she'd said.

"Susan Rogers, I better not hear that language out of your mouth again," Emmett scolded. "Is that the kind of language you use with your friends?"

"You're not my parent. You've been gone a long time Emmett. Times have changed and so have I," Suzy answered sticking out her tongue at Emmett.

"Jason cheated on me? When and with whom?" Paula asked looking devastated.

Emmett gave a hard look to Suzy.

"Sorry Emmett." then turned to her sister she said, "I shouldn't have said that."

"You tell me right now Suzy, or I swear I'm going to pull out all your hair."

Emmett glared at Suzy and shook his head, but Suzy answered anyway, "Fine, but remember you asked me. Jason slept with Nancy Graham this morning."

"This morning? Really? And Nancy? That skank?" Paula looked angry and then composing herself said calmly, "We did break-up, so I can forgive him, if he wanted me back."

"If he wanted you back? But...,"Suzy cried.

The front door of the apartment opened and in Jason walked.

"I heard that Paula and you've got to let me explain...I'm so sorry. I was so hurt that I wanted to hurt you back, baby. Nancy is a skank. She's not you. You're worth ten of her!! I thought you hated me and that is why you broke up with me. I'm done with the drugs. I even got a job so I can support you and the baby."

"You know about the baby? How?"

"Suzy told me this morning. Marry me Paula, I love you and I'll make a great dad I promise."

"This is really sudden, and you were with Nancy this morning."

"I told you she means nothing. You and that baby are my world now and for the future."

"Get out of here Jason, or I'm calling the cops. I didn't invite you in my apartment. You're trespassing," Frannie shouted.

"If he leaves, I leave," Paula responded.

"Don't do anything rash Paula. You can take your time. Come stay with Jenna and me and then decide what you want to do," Emmett begged.

"Do you even have a place yet?" Paula asked.

"Actually I do. My friend Paul offered us shelter until I find us a permanent place."

"Don't listen to him Paula, you can come stay with my mother and I," Jason demanded.

"Jason, you have to give me some time. You were with Nancy this morning. How do I know you even mean any of this?"

"But I do mean it. I have a job now. I can support us all... three of us."

"I know you think you do Jason, but I have the baby to consider. Give me a few days."

"Fine, but you have to promise you won't let your brother convince you not to marry me. I can tell he doesn't like me."

"Emmett may be my brother, but I make my own decisions. Emmett tell Jason, where I will be."

"Paula, I don't think this is a good idea," Emmett protested.

"Emmett if you want me to leave with you then you must tell Jason where I will be."

"Fine! We will be at One Thousand Trails End. Call first. Here's my cell number," Emmett replied handing him a piece of paper with a cell number.

"I love you Paula so I'll give you a couple of days then I'm coming for you and my child," Jason replied as he left the apartment.

Emmett flagged a cab and putting Suzy and Paula in first he then climbed in giving the address to the cabbie. He watched as Jason got in his car and drove away. Emmett wasn't sorry he'd given Jason a fake number. He was worried how Paula would react when she found out the address was fake too. He would deal with that when it came to that. He only hoped that keeping Jason away would make him more appealing.

~0~

Chapter 3 - Flashback

Emmett awoke disoriented, for moment he thought he was in Afghanistan; but he then realized he slept on the *La-Z-Boy* chair. He was at his friend Paul's. It was the middle of the night, the air was brisk and he had only slept about two hours. He glanced over at the pullout bed, where Suzy and Paula were sleeping; grateful he hadn't woke them, though he was sure he had shouted in his sleep.

Suzy hadn't wanted to detach herself from Paula, so he had called his mom and gotten permission for Suzy to stay overnight. Jenna would join them later today, after they went shopping for two beds. He needed to find an apartment as well, or Jenna would be miserable. He and Jenna couldn't share the same room as his sister.

He scrambled to think of anything else he could think about. This exercise wasn't working, even though he tried to think of other things his dreams of Afghanistan left him shaken. He was right back to where he had been after the incident. Why couldn't he put this behind him? Other soldiers had been through things like this and moved on. He'd undergone therapy; he done his penance; why couldn't he just erase all of this from his mind like it never happened. Because it had and he couldn't change any of it so he had to accept what happened and move on. If only it were that easy! His thoughts went back to that day that began it all.

Cadet Officer Tommy Harrow always a screw-up with the recklessness of youth had disobeyed orders and gone into town. Tommy had recently been assigned to their squad and had not adapting well. Tommy was brash, and fool hearty twenty year old who acted like a kid, Hell; he was called the kid by the others some like Emmet who weren't much older than him accept in experience. Tommy always ventured in where others feared to tread which to some made him the ideal soldier; but he also had no impulse control which made him persona non grata with others. Tommy never seemed to want to obey orders. He nodded and appeared to hear the orders, then do everything his own way. Of course Tommy had a winning personality; he could wheedle and finagle his way getting supplies and getting out of scrapes so easily it seemed he was charmed. Emmett however had he coaxed Tommy's last posting details and had read of how Tommy though to have been responsible for leading his unit into enemy territory.

The captain seemed to think Tommy was a burnt out, but burnt out, or not, Tommy was a risk to their unit. His careless attitude made them all worry. They had taken to keeping an eye out for Tommy's action to protect their unit and Tommy.

That day Tommy had disappeared on regular patrol. As the squad searched for him, they were told by some children that Tommy had dishonored Raishma Wahidi by being seen with her without a male of her family and without her ḥijāb. One child said this meant she had dishonored her family and their god, for a woman wore this to keep her hair and neck veiled from males who were not family.

Two days went by as they searched for Tommy and the young woman. Raishma Wahidi was found dead, stripped of all her clothes and all her flesh burned; only the remains of her clothing and some bones were found. No evidence was found of Tommy.

Tommy had been warned of fraternizing with Afghan women but he seemed he hadn't learned and now it looked like some Afghan men had taken him to punish him. Tommy had been warned of fraternizing with Afghan women, but he seemed he hadn't learned and now it looked like some Afghan men had taken him to punish him.

Emmett's, Captain Campbell hoped they would be able to bargain with the men, to get Tommy back. Perhaps even promise, that Tommy would marry the disgraced woman if need be, to keep the peace. Emmett hoped that would work; but Tommy was a westerner and some tribes didn't like their woman to marry outside their religion.

Captain Campbell and the team had approached the elders of the village hoping to secure Tommy's release, only to find themselves surrounded by Taliban sympathizers and taken for questioning. The five men left in the squad had been captured.

Emmett could almost feel the slow torture, which they had done to him; as his mind went back to that time. First they condemned them all for Tommy's actions with Raishma Wahidi. They insinuated that troops had come to rape the land and the women. Westerners were despised and the damage to some areas had been blamed on the soldiers whether they were responsible or not. At first it was just questions fired at them and then it was a denial of food and water. They had then separated the unit, person by person; but not so they couldn't hear each other being tortured. The Taliban sympathizers had then demanded troop information and anything else they knew about the Canadian government's plans.

Emmett wouldn't give in and that made them angry. Three days of torture, no food, no water, just tiny strips of skin, tore off his back with a lash, as he screamed in anguish under a black hood. The last torturer had beaten Emmett with his fists, leaving bruises throughout his body, but Emmett wouldn't give up any information.

It seemed like days of unending pain where he had found a corner of his mind to hide in. In that corner he could see Happy Valley, his sisters and his family and they were all happy. His interrogator couldn't take that from him. His oppressor thought him bruised and beaten to broken to talk when he left and promising to return in a few hours to finish up the job. His torturer ordered him taken back to the prison room chair and all. Emmett pretended to be unconscious and they set the chair in and left quickly. Emmett had the impression that they were afraid to be found with him dead. Did they really think he would die here? They were wrong!

Emmett drew on his last bit of strength. He didn't know where his Captain had been taken, or where they had his lieutenant, so it was up to him to take charge and save his troops...save them all. Especially as he overheard one of his captors say they were bringing in a new torturer, '*the Knife*'. Rumour in spy circles in Afghanistan said that this man was ruthless. The' *Knife's'* tactics always succeeded; his known methods of slowly skinning someone alive obtained the highest amount of information. He wouldn't allow his unit to fall prey to this evil animal.

Emmett despite the beatings; had been thinking on how to escape the bindings on his hands and feet. By working carefully, he managed to tear a strip of metal off the chair they placed him in, when he returned from the torture room. He waited for sounds of the enemy, then hearing none; he used this piece of metal to cut the plastic strip that held his hands and feet. Emmett pulled the hood from his eyes and looked around when he was free. He found a shirt discarded in the corner and put the shirt on his sore back.

Emmett scanned the dimly room to find that of his five membered recon squad, only two besides Emmett were in this room; one of those severely injured, lay prone on the floor, not moving. The other, his lieutenant, insisted he could escape despite his wounds. Emmett wasn't so sure but they had to chance it for if they stayed they could all die.

Emmett scanned the room searching for a guard. There were none in the room. Emmett cut the bonds from the two men, and then scanned to find out where the sentries were. He had counted when they took him to the torture area and knew that it was at least fifty steps away. He had heard at least three voices. So possibly three men guarded them? Emmett peered outside the doorway carefully keeping from being seen.

A sentry posted just outside seemed to be sleeping at the door. Emmett crept outside the room and encircled the man with his arm. The sentry's eyes snapped open with surprise, and with one smooth movement, before he could even cry out, Emmett snapped the man's neck.

Emmett grabbed the man's side arm and tucked that in his waistband. Emmett's neck tingled; but he knew it was his lieutenant at his back and he didn't turn. Lieutenant 'Fred' Fadil Aswad made signs with his hands on Emmett's back. Emmett knew his lieutenant's hand signs distinguished what this meant. The lieutenant had heard someone coming, time to set up an ambush. Emmett and Lieutenant Aswad pulled the dead man into the room where they had been held captive. Then they waited on either side of the door, for the person they could hear coming. The man stepped into the room and whispered, "Second Lieutenant Rogers?"

"You're lucky we didn't take you out Officer Cadet Harrow," Emmett replied.

"You wouldn't have done that, would you have, Emmett?"

"If the Lieutenant had ordered me to I would have followed through with the order," Emmett admitted.

"And here I came to rescue you," Tommy laughed.

"That's funny because we wouldn't be even in this position if you hadn't disobeyed orders," Emmett complained.

"I know Lieutenant Rogers, but I'm trying to make it right. I think I know where they holding the Captain."

"Where?" asked Lieutenant Aswad.

"They're holding him two buildings over towards the field," Tommy answered.

"You're bleeding Harrow. Where are you injured?" Emmett asked.

"Took a bullet to the side... just a little bleeding, but I don't think it hit any organs. I'll be fine. I took out two sentries so it should be smooth sailing. There are two trucks outside, one with keys. I can help you rescue Captain Campbell."

"Two sentries? If anyone discovers that, we will be sitting ducks, "Emmett answered.

"Draw me a map Harrow, so I can go rescue the Captain," Lieutenant Aswad commanded. "You will go with Second Lieutenant Rogers and take and Officer Cadet Mancini to the truck and get him to medics."

Emmett stared hard at his lieutenant and realized he was in no shape to retrieve the captain. Lieutenant Aswad was more severely beaten then the rest of them. His eyes were almost swollen shut and what skin revealed in the tears in his shirt, was purple and raised. His left leg had a bone sticking out of his torn pants.

"Sir, with all due respect, you should allow me to handle rescuing the Captain. I am the least injured and these men need you to take them to safety," Emmett interjected.

"Do you question my commands, Second Lieutenant Rogers?"

"Yes, sir, I believe that you need medical attention just as much as Harrow and Mancini. Do you really believe you can rescue the Cap on your own?"

"Do you believe you can rescue him, Emmett? You're injured too. Your eye looks nasty and your arm looks ragged and bruised."

"Nothing a little rest and recreation would fix. When get back maybe they'll let us take a trip to the beach? I'm certainly going to try and succeed sir, if you allow me to do complete the mission."

"Yes, I'd love a trip to the beach right now Emmett, but first we need to get out of this hell Emmett. All of us!! I don't like leaving this all up to you," Lieutenant Aswad.

"You were going to do it on your own," Emmett pointed out.

"Proceed then and good luck."

"Aw, Second Loo, let me help. I don't want to stay with him," Tommy complained, in whispers to Emmett motioning with his hands that the lieutenant was the enemy.

"That's Lieutenant Aswad to you, Cadet. You have already put your squad at risk by not adhering to the rules I am not about to put up with your ethnic slurs. You will address your superior officer with respect and you will follow his orders. Am I clear?" Emmett demanded.

"Yes, sir, Lieutenant Rogers, but aren't you worried he's one of them?"

"I repeat Lieutenant 'Fred' Fadil Aswad is your superior. He has been vetted for his position and he is a loyal Canadian. You have put us in the position where your fellow officers are injured. Who is the problem here? Don't think you won't hear about this when we are back on base. You have disobeyed a superior's orders for the last time. Now you will follow orders, Lieutenant Aswad's orders as if it was the Captain, or me giving them is that clear?"

"Yes, sir, Second Lieutenant Rogers," Tommy replied a sarcastic lilt to his voice.

Lieutenant Aswad smiled at Emmett, and then gave Tommy a stink eye.

"Lieutenant Aswad if he gives you any trouble; I'd shoot him!" Emmett quipped.

"He doesn't mean that Lieutenant Aswad," Tommy replied worried.

"Just follow my orders and we'll never have to find out. Will we?" Aswad commented narrowing his swollen eyes so they looked like slits.

Aswad then turned to Emmett and his eyes showed this was all a joke, but Tommy saw none of this. Emmett helped them as far as the doorway, to the entrance where the two trucks were parked. Going across the courtyard, he followed the directions on the map to the building, where they were holding Captain Campbell.

He ducked behind a rusty truck just in time, as he saw the glint of a rifle. An Afghan man stood in front of the doorway Emmett needed to pass to get into the building. Emmett waited watching the man, trying to format a plan to sneak by him. The man put his head down and pulled out a package of cigarettes. He then began searching for a light. Finding no matches the man entered the building leaving the coast clear. Emmett advanced, slipping in the building unnoticed.

Emmett heard the sound of footsteps, echoing on the cement floor and he opened the door of the first room hiding there. His heart pounded as he feared discovery; but he continued picking the lock with the wire he had kept and then looked around the room. It appeared to be an office with charts and Emmett quickly gathered what he could and hid them, beneath his shirt to carry them away. In the desk drawer he found a gun and keys, which he recognized belonged to an old truck, just like the one he had seen outside. He placed the keys in his pocket and tucked the gun in his waistband.

Grabbing a pillow from the chair he took that too. Emmett heard the clicking of the doorknob and then heard more footsteps walking away. Emmett waited a few minutes, and then went down the hall towards where Tommy said the captain would be. He slowed as he came to where the hall curved hearing voices up ahead.

"Why are you here? Where are your troops situated?" Emmett heard.

"Captain Robert Campbell of the Canadian army Serial number X12 345 678."

Emmett heard a weird noise and moaning. He wanted to just move in, but he had to make sure there was only one man there first; hopefully his captain would remain alive until then. Emmett advanced slowly, and quietly, like the cat they had nicknamed him after. He peered into the room, seeing only one man beside Captain Campbell. Captain Campbell hooded except for his mouth, had no shirt on. In the man's hands a knife and a strip of flesh he had skinned from the captain's back. His back was layered with lash marks as well. Emmett fired through the pillow killing the man.
"You can't scare me even if you've changed tactics, *Knife.* Take all the skin you want I won't tell you anything but my name rank and serial number," Captain Campbell shouted, in response.

"It's me, captain; it's Second Lieutenant Rogers," Emmett explained as he removed the hood and bent down to untie the captain's hands and feet.

"Thank the heaven's it's you. Do you know where the other men are?" asked Captain Campbell.

"Lieutenant Aswad, Officers Harrow and Mancini are on their way back to base and medics sir."

"How bad are they?"

"Lieutenant Aswad is in pretty bad shape sir; severely beaten, more so than the other two. Harrow has some bruising and a through and through in his side and Mancini is concussed and bruised," Emmett answered. "I can't find Officer Cadet Bowman."

"Bowman is dead," Captain Campbell confessed.

Emmett was taken aback by this but he hid this; he had a job to do. He would put fears and grief aside and do the task at hand.

"And how are you Rogers? You look pretty banged up yourself."

"Just bruised sir, I can get us out of here. Here's a weapon sir. Can you walk?"

"Yes."

Captain Campbell stood up and nearly collapsed.

"Lean on me cap," Emmett urged.

Emmett then proceeded to take the captain down the hall, to the door Emmett had come in. Near the door, Emmett propped the captain against a wall and then snuck up behind the man smoking. He placed his arm around the man's neck and snapped it. He then grabbed the captain's arm and walked through the door, placing the captain on his right side. Looking for snipers, he hurried across the courtyard to the old truck he had seen. He was sure the keys he had found would start the truck.

Emmett had almost reached the truck, when he felt three stings as bullets hit first his leg, then his shoulder. One bullet bounced off his head, grazing him. Emmett managed to get to the truck and help the captain inside. He noted the gas tank gauge was at F. Emmett was sure he knew how far they were away and which way it was to the base. They would make it back to the base and help if he could just get the truck started.

The captain now bleeding from his side needed medical attention. Emmett took off his shirt, leaning over he covered the captain's wound to stop the bleeding. The captain took over holding pressure on the wound as Emmett started the truck and drove at high speed before pursuers could catch them. Emmett hoped the gas gauge was correct and they could make it back to the base before the gas ran out or the captain succumbed from his injuries. He also hoped that Tommy had gotten all the other men back as well. Time would tell. Emmett put his foot harder on the gas and increased his speed. It was then he saw Tommy's over turned truck up ahead. He only hoped they were still alive as it looked like they had hit a landmine.

Emmett fought a bad headache obviously the bullet that had struck his head had caused some damage. It didn't help that his sunglasses were obscuring some of his sight. Emmett brushed then then realized he wasn't wearing any sunglasses. Okay, he could deal with this. The headache made his left eye have tunnel vision. Calmness took over Emmett; he could still see therefore he could save his men from the overturned truck.

Emmett stopped his truck to assess the scene. First he checked his captain's wound. Some of the bleeding had stopped in Captain Campbell's wound; was that good or bad? He wasn't sure. Officer Cadet Helen Bowman had been the medic and Captain Campbell said she was dead. Somehow even before he uttered the words Emmett had known that the captain would say Helen was dead.

The Taliban had issued a decree that any female that, by any means, plays a role in the war against *mujahideen* should be killed. The *muhahideen* being the "holy warriors" the Taliban called themselves. So confusing the two terms so close in spelling and sound. It all seemed a lot of bullshit to Emmett. Exactly why they thought it was okay to dictate everything women could do and think Emmett didn't know; but he knew that's part of what this fight was all about. The Taliban were not only terrorist but they advocated what amounted to hate, and even more than just misogyny in Emmett's mind Helen had wanted these woman to have the right to speak and advocate for themselves and that's why she too had joined the army.

Helen hadn't stood a chance. Emmett knew people considered it sexist, but he had felt women should not be in combat. They were more vulnerable and at greater risk just because the enemy would use their sex to achieve greater damage to their foe. Emmett had treated Bowman like one of the men and now she was dead. Emmett wished she had stayed behind at the base, instead of insisting on finding Tommy; but didn't that make him misogynistic? He was dictating how women should live...that was wrong too.

"I'm okay Emmett, Go! See how the men are," ordered Captain Campbell.

Emmett exited the cab of the truck searching for his men. He found Lieutenant Aswad dead; half of his body in one spot, the other half in another. He found Cadet Officer Harrow unconscious by the roadside.

"Lieutenant Aswad is dead, isn't he?" Tommy asked, "And Pete Mancini?"

"Yes, Lieutenant Aswad is dead. Pete is injured but if we get him some help he'll survive," Emmett admitted.
"I'm sorry Emmett. This is my fault. I know I'm a screw-up. Just take Mancini. Don't bother with me."

"Hush, Tommy. I'll get you fixed up, and Mancini's coming too," Emmett soothed.

Tommy's legs were still attached, but were mostly bone left with little flesh to cover them. Emmett tied off the left leg which profusely bled above the knee with his belt. Then he ripped a section of his pants to tie off Tommy's other leg. He only hoped he wasn't too late and that Tommy hadn't lost too much blood. He then carried Tommy firefighter style to the truck cab. He covered Tommy with an old blanket he found in the cab hoping it wasn't so dirty it would infect the wounds.

Cadet Officer Mancini was burnt almost beyond recognition. Emmett was afraid to touch him he was burnt so badly, but it was obvious he needed help immediately or he would die. Emmett carefully lifted him and put him in the back of the truck. He begged Mancini not to die as he heard a rattle in his chest. He then put him carefully into the back of the truck beside Tommy Harrow.

"Give him the blanket Emmett, he needs it worse," Tommy demanded, attempting to give the blanket to Mancini.

"We will make it Emmett," Captain Campbell reassured Emmett, as he got back in the truck.

"I know we'll make it Captain, it's not far now," Emmett agreed, and then prayed that he was right as he started the truck.

Emmett drove down the road a piece, until he hit a rut in the road. The jolt of the bump had made him hit his head on the truck roof and Emmett now found himself unable to see out of his left eye. Not only that, but his headache had gotten worse. He glanced down briefly with his good eye to see that his leg had stopped bleeding from what he thought an insignificant wound. His shoulder however bled profusely. He couldn't let a little thing like temporary blindness, or a little blood stop him, the men were depending on him. He had to keep driving until he made it to the base, so he willed himself to succeed.

Emmett drove for some time and then realized the sentry point was up ahead. They would make it. He slowed down and identified himself, telling the sentries what had happened. One of the sentries, climbed in pushing Emmett over beside his captain, and drove the truck. Emmett had done all he could, the rest was up to God. Emmett closed his eyes in relief and allowed himself to pass out.

~0~

E mmett awoke his head pounding. Where was he and why couldn't he see out of his eyes? His hands went up to his eyes, where he found a bandage. Why did he have a bandage on his eyes and head?

"Second Lieutenant Rogers are you awake?" a soft female voice enquired.

"Where am I?" Emmett asked.

"You are at the base hospital in Kandahar."

"Afghanistan," Emmett stated.

"Yes."

"We were on routine patrol when someone snatched Tommy," Emmett stated, remembering the story they had all agreed to tell.

"You rescued Tommy, Aswad, Mancini and Captain Campbell. Do you remember that?"

"Of course, I remember. Don't ask me stupid questions. Lieutenant Aswad died when Tommy hit a landmine," Emmett shouted and then regretted it because it made his head hurt.

"Tommy's my brother," the voice said quietly.

"I'm sorry. My head aches but I shouldn't have yelled at you. Will Tommy be okay?"

"He seems better. They flew him to Germany. They've been updating me."

"They wouldn't let you go to him?" Emmett asked.

"I won't tell anyone; but Tommy knew he could trust me with the real story before they flew him out of here. I maybe a nurse here but I'm also in the military. I can't just leave, besides I promised Tommy I'd look after you.

"You didn't really answer my question," Emmett stated.

"I don't want to upset you. The doctor ordered you be kept calm."

"Then tell me what happened to what is left of my squad or I won't be calm!" Emmett replied.

"Tommy's lost both his legs, but they think he'll be fine in time."

"And Officer Mancini, and Captain Campbell?"

"Captain Campbell took a bullet through his side that ricocheted through his body. He had a collapsed lung, nicked liver and kidney and a lacerated spleen."

"But he's going to be okay?" Emmett demanded.

"They patched him up and flew him to Germany. He's not completely out of the woods, but they believe he'll survive."

"Mancini died?" guessed Emmett

"Yes," the woman confirmed. "Officer Pete Mancini died three days after you brought him here. He had burns on almost ninety percent of his body. You couldn't save him Emmett," the woman comforted, as Emmett began to sob.

"You've upset my patient," a man admonished the doctor, standing nearby "I told you that you could look after my patient only if you didn't upset him."

"I'm sorry."

"I'm fine," Emmett replied pulling himself together, embarrassed that he had cried so openly.

"No, you are not Second Lieutenant Rogers, but you will be," the doctor replied.

Emmett felt a warm coursing in his veins as the doctor injected something into his intravenous in his hand.

"Did he ask about his own injuries?" the doctor enquired, as Emmett felt himself grow sleepy.

"No," Tommy's sister answered.

"Tell me," Emmett muttered fighting the drug.

"You'll be okay Emmett. You're a brave man. You had a blood clot on the brain. We've fixed that."

"The truck," mumbled Emmett remembering, "My eyes."

"We fixed a blood clot behind your eye and you should be able to get the bandages off tomorrow. The brass can't believe how you laboured; getting all the men in the truck and then driving with no eyesight in your left eye, a blood clot getting bigger by the moment. It must have been like something dangling in front of your eyes, the whole time. You had a collapsed lung and a severed artery in your leg, but I do good work and that's all fixed. That's right, rest give in. Emmett we will talk later." The doctor reassured as Emmett felt himself slip under again.

Emmett's thoughts slipped back into present day and found himself in a ball in the closet. How had he gotten here? He had allowed the memories to overwhelm him and takeover his body. Memories should be left neatly in the past. Forgotten! He had survived he couldn't allow these recollections to break him. He wouldn't allow it. He knew that he had hidden some of the memories of the torture even from himself, but he wouldn't allow himself to remember them and harm his psyche. Emmett glanced over at Paula still sleeping. His sisters needed him he would be their big brother again. Paula needed help he could do that. His dad needed to take responsibility for his behaviour. He would convince his mom to leave his dad if he didn't change.

"Emmett, are you okay?" Suzy asked, suddenly at his shoulder.

"I'm fine, Suzy-que."

"But you're in a closet..."
"I'm fine."
"I'm sorry. I know we've all put you under more stress. I know what happened in Afghanistan..," Suzy began.

"Did Jenna tell you?" Emmett asked surprised.

"Actually when they called they asked for Jenna or Mom. Jenna wasn't home and Mom was in bed sick, so I pretended to be Jenna. They told me how you saved those soldiers and that you were hurt."

"They told you?" Emmett asked.

"They told me you were tortured Emmett," Suzy admitted reluctantly.

"They shouldn't have told you. What did mom say?"

"I didn't tell mom or anyone. Mom has been so sick from the chemo and I didn't want to worry her when they said you'd be okay."

"What about Jenna?"

"I didn't tell Jenna, because she didn't seem interested in any news about you. Sorry Emmett, but you asked," Suzy explained.

"Then you told dad?"

"No, he's been sick too. I don't know what's wrong with him but he's been going to the doctor. He's says it's the price of getting older, so I don't think it's serious."

"But mom is sick? I thought she beat the breast cancer."

"We all thought she had, but she's had a re-occurrence of the cancer. She has been going for chemo, like I said."

"Then Mom will be fine she's beaten it once she can do it again."

"Yes, we can only hope so. But about what happened to you..."

"I want some coffee."

"You're avoiding the subject Emmett. You need to get help for what happened to you. Have you been able to talk about it? I understand that is important as well as some drug therapies."

"How do you know anything about this? You shouldn't be worried about me. You are sixteen-years- old. You should be having fun and dating. I'm going to be fine," Emmett reassured her.

"Emmett unless you get help it will get worse. I read up about this on the internet," Suzy cautioned.

"I have a shrink. Don't worry Suzy-que. I won't let this get the best of me. Just let me settle Paula in our apartment and then I promise I'll get some more help."

"I don't think you should be starting work next week Emmett you need some time off. Can't you ask if you can start in say... six months? Blame family troubles but take some time Emmett you need it."

"I don't know if they'd do that..."

"Try okay for me," Suzy begged.

"Okay just don't tell anyone about this."

"Emmett you don't need to be embarrassed. This isn't a weakness on your part. You were tortured and you still managed to save your men."

"Not all of them..."

"No, one could have Emmett."

"I'm sorry for worry you Suzy, now what would you like for breakfast? I could go to the McDonald's down the street and get us some *Egg Mcmuffins*. Paula still likes them right?"

"Yes, Paula likes them. You better get her some pancakes too. She's been really hungry lately," Suzy advised.

"Okay, do you want some too Suzy?"

"They are loaded with calories but the *Egg Mcmuffin* will be sufficient."

Emmett then went into the bathroom and threw on his clothes exiting he exclaimed, "See you in a while Suzy."

~0~

Emmett enjoyed the simple breakfast with his sisters. It was so good to be with them again. So many times he had wished he was here when in Afghanistan. He had missed simple family interaction. He had missed Jenna too. Emmett thought back to the conversation he had with Jenna on the way to the McDonald's. Jenna had first complained that Emmett had woke her, and then said she wouldn't come to live with him until he had a real apartment. Obviously Jenna wasn't happy with him and she had cause. He would have to show her how much she meant to him. Paula telling him that Jenna too had strayed made his guilt feelings a lot easier.

Helen Bowman had been a sweet woman he had to leave her in the past. He grieved that he hadn't been able to save her, but he had to move on from that situation. Everything complemented, that is what worked for him. Emmett had a wife and he made vows to Jenna. He couldn't keep thinking about a woman who was dead, no matter how much she had meant to him. As for Jenna going out with other men, how could he be angry with her when he too had been attracted to someone? It wasn't like either of them had slept with anyone else. Though thinking about someone else appeared a form of cheating. No! He was home now. He would be a better husband and perhaps they could be parents? He wanted a family of his own and he knew Jenna did too, so maybe they could both work towards it. If they hadn't lost the baby they wouldn't have strayed. Emmett would make things right with Jenna and then all would be right with his world.

"Emmett I have to go home and get a change of clothes," Suzy stated interrupting Emmett's thoughts.

"Oh, sorry, Suzy. Do you need some cash for a cab to go home and then get to school?"

"Will you talk to me outside, Emmett?" Suzy asked.

"Go talk with Suzy, Emmett. I'm going back to bed anyway. I haven't been sleeping well. You should go see Jenna, anyway," Paula said.

"Okay, see you later, Paula," Emmett replied. He then stepped outside with Suzy.

"I thought maybe you could come home with me and then go to the parent teacher conference at eleven a.m.

There's no school today," Suzy explained.

"Why isn't mom or dad going?" Emmett asked.

"Mom and Dad both have doctor appointments this morning."

"Why didn't they reschedule?"

"I didn't ask them to. Mom needs to go to this appointment I think she's hoping for good news," Suzy explained.

"Will it be okay if your brother comes to the conference then?"

"Yes, at least someone is coming," Suzy stated.

"Are you okay at school Suzy?"

"Yes," Suzy answered, but it appeared obvious to Emmett that she lied.

Emmett rolled his eyes at her.

"Okay, so my grades slipped a little but I'm working to make them up. I'm not failing; I'm just getting B's."

"I'm sorry Suzy; it must have been rough on you with no one here for you. You knew Paula was pregnant for a long time, didn't you?"

"Yes, it's not like Paula could tell mom. Mom has been really sick and has enough to worry about," Suzy explained.

"What about Dad?"

"Dad has never gone to my school and if I had asked him he would have yelled at me about my grades. I really tried Emmett."

"I know Suzy. It's going to be okay now, your big brother came home, and I'm going to help," Emmett offered.

"I know Emmett; it's great to have you home again. I missed you, bro."

"I missed you too."

Chapter 4 - What Doesn' t Destroy Me

Emmett and Suzy took the cab to his parent's home.

Emmett asked the cab to wait as Suzy went in and quickly changed. Emmett and Suzy arrived at the school and Emmett saw all her teachers. Emmett explained all that Suzy had been through and her teachers were sympathetic. They offered to give her extra credit work to make her report cards reflect A's again. Suzy seemed angry with him as they left the school and got in the taxi. Emmett gave the address for his parent's home to the taxi driver and then turned to Suzy.

"Why are you angry with me Suzy?"

"When I asked you to go see my teachers I didn't think you'd embarrass me."

"How did I embarrass you?" Emmett asked surprised.

"You told them our family secrets."

"What's wrong with that?" Emmett enquired.

"It's no one's business, but our family. You know what mom and dad say keep family business to ourselves. I haven't told anyone how you hide in closets."

"My situation is different and I need to deal with it in my way. Yours affected your school work. I needed to tell your teachers so they could cut you so slack."

"I wish you hadn't told them. Now people will look on me with sympathy," Suzy complained as the taxi arrived at their parent's home.

Emmett paid the cab driver and got out. Looking up he surprised to see a police vehicle in the driveway and a policeman knocking at their front door. Emmett took Suzy hand and kept her behind him as they approached the front door.

"Do you live here?" asked the officer.

"Yes," Suzy answered.

"Names please," asked the officer.

"I am Emmett Rogers, and this is my sister, Susan Rogers. Why are you here? Has something happened?" Emmett asked not really wanting to know the answer.

"Emmett Rogers? You're supposed to start on the force next week. Just got back from Afghanistan right?"

"That is correct. Is that why you are here?" Emmett asked, relaxing.

"Can we do this inside Mr. Rogers?"

"Just tell us." Emmett demanded.

"I am sorry to tell you this but Matilda and Tobias Rogers were in a car accident last night."

"We need to go to them then," Suzy stated then turning to Emmett she said. "Right, Emmett?"

Emmett saw the officer face change and he knew the truth, even before he said it.

"I'm sorry Miss Rogers, Mr. Rogers. I'm sorry to tell you this, but Matilda and Tobias Rogers were killed instantly, when Tobias Rogers lost control of his car and crossed the centre line hitting a guard rail on the other side."

"Thank you for coming at this difficult time, officer," Emmett retorted, as Suzy started crying loudly.

Emmett took Suzy in his arms and took her into the house sitting her in a kitchen chair. The police officer followed them to ask some questions and then left. Emmett then made Suzy hot chocolate which he put in her hand.

"What will we do Emmett? I'm under eighteen; they'll take me away," Suzy asked, as she sipped the drink.

"No one will take you Suzy. I'm your brother. I won't let anyone take you. I'll get guardianship and look after you," Emmett promised.

"Emmett, I think he did it on purpose."

"You think Dad did it on purpose?"

"I know he did. I found this yesterday," Suzy said as she handed Emmett a piece of paper. "Dad had prostate cancer."

"Why didn't you tell me?"

"You had enough to worry about with mom and Paula and your health problems."

"I have no health problems," Emmett denied and then continued, "Even Dad wouldn't have done this on purpose. I'm sure you're mistaken."

Emmett thought about he wasn't so sure his dad couldn't have done this on purpose but he couldn't let Suzy know that. It would be just like the selfish bastard to kill himself and mom and not think of the consequences. Emmett remembered when he was young his father had illustrated how he could easily take a life when he had killed the cat. His father had tapped the cat on the head with a shovel because it was sick. Yes the man could have done this.

"Will you be okay here for a half an hour, while I go get Paula?" Emmett asked.

"Yes, you should go tell her in person and bring her home," Suzy agreed.

Emmett called a cab and then went to get Paula. Emmett let himself into the basement apartment to find Paula watching television and laughing at something on the Live with Regis and Kelly show. How could he tell her?

"You're back sooner than I thought. Did you see Jenna yet?"

"No, I went home with Suzy and...," Emmett hesitated.

"Emmett what's wrong?" asked Paula.

"I don't know how to say this other than to say it. Mom and Dad were in an accident..."

"Then we should go to them."

"We can't Paula. I'm sorry they are dead."

"I don't believe you. Why did you make this up? If this is a ploy to keep me from Jason it's won't work. Don't think that I don't know you gave Jason the wrong address and phone number," Paula sniped.

"I'm so sorry Paula. I'm not. I wish to God I was."

"What? You're wrong! Tell me you're lying to me Emmett. Please."

"Paula, I'm sorry I lied to Jason. If I'm honest I don't think he's good enough for you, but I wouldn't lie about this."

"How did it happen?"

"The police officer said Dad lost control of the car crossed the centre line and hit the guard rail on the other side," Emmett explained.

"Dad did it, didn't he? The son of bitch killed her. I tried to get her to leave him but she kept saying I can't. I love him and now he's killed her."

Paula cried then broke into huge sobs her belly shaking with each one. Emmett hugged his sister as tightly as he could without crushing her burgeoning belly and tried his best to comfort her.

After a few minutes Paula composed herself and asked "Does Suzy know?"

"Yes, but she needs us to be with her," Emmett insisted.

"When has she ever needed anyone? Suzy is self-sufficient."

"Is she? Or does she pretend? She's just a kid, Paula."

"And I'm not?" Paula responded.

"You've still got some growing up to do but you're going to be a mother, Paula."

"I know and sometimes I still can't believe it."

"I'm going to be there to help you, Paula."

"That all really nice, but things have changed Emmett. I don't need you. Jason will be there for me."

"You don't have to live with Jason. I'll take care of us all," Emmett pleaded.

"I love Jason. He's not perfect; but he's the father of my baby, so you better get used to him. He'll be around for good. If I have to choose I'll choose him." Paula insisted.

"We can talk about this later. Right now we have to get back to Suzy."

"Fine, but this discussion isn't over," Paula announced.

Two days later at six am. Emmett couldn't believe how fast the funeral had gone. Jenna had cried and then pitched in helping with funeral arrangements. Jenna had been a huge help herding people to the wake and getting his sisters drinks. It was wonderful to have his Jenna back. People they had seen in years came to the funeral.

It still seemed unreal that his parents were gone. He would look out of the corner of his eye and expect to see his mother sitting at the kitchen table drinking her tea. He felt guilty at how little he missed his father. Memories of how many times he excused his father's behaviour when as a child had flooded his mind the last few days.

Father? The man wasn't worthy of the title. From now on he would think of him, if he thought of him at all would be Tobias. He started thinking maybe Paula, Suzy and himself could be happier, without Tobias Rogers in their lives. He just wished the sick, selfish bastard hadn't taken their mother too. Even if she had been sick and dying they should have had that time with her and Tobias had stolen it all away.

He had heard Suzy crying the last three nights, when she didn't think they could hear her. He wanted to help her, but he didn't know how. All he could do was tell her he'd be there for her and that he loved her. Was that enough? As for Paula she was more withdrawn. She barely spoke to either of them. Emmett was glad she at least stayed in the family home. She had gone off a few times with Jason, the last couple of days, but slept at home.

Emmett had seen a lawyer yesterday, who started the paper work for Emmett to retain custody of his sister Suzy. The lawyer looked happier, after seeing his father's will. His father taken out a life insurance policy a year ago, that would also help with expenses provided they paid up given the circumstances of his death. The police had called it an accident, so maybe the insurance company wouldn't fight it. Emmett hoped so since he had spoken with the police department, and got a six month extension before he would start. They would need the money. Tobias left a will granting custody to Emmett along with most of his money and their home, provided he looked after Suzy until she was twenty-one, so the lawyer thought custody would be a formality; one less problem for Emmett to worry about.

The dreams still kept coming, however and Emmett found himself sleeping walking. Yesterday he had found himself in bare feet in the backyard at two a.m., wondering how he had gotten there. He remembered dreaming about looking for someone, and then he dreamt he was back in Afghanistan. Hell, he hadn't even cried, he was tough and he would remain strong. He couldn't let these dreams get the best of them though his sisters needed him.

Oh no, he almost forgotten today was Paula's birthday maybe Suzy could help him plan a birthday party for her with all her friends. He'd even invite Jason since that would make Paula happy.

"Emmett we need to talk," Jenna insisted.

"What about Jenna?" Emmett asked not really wanting to know.

"Don't play games Emmett. You've been gone a long time and things have changed. I'm older wiser and not the little girl you married at eighteen."

"You want a divorce?"

"Do you?" Jenna asked.

"No. But you do, don't you?"

"I'd like to try again Emmett but I can't stay at home and just be your wife. I want a career," Jenna admitted.

"What is it you want to do?"

"I want to go to nursing school," Jenna admitted.

"Done when does the term start?"

"The course begins next week."

"We have some money left from my stint in the army; why don't you use that and go back to school, just give them a cheque and enroll."

"That's exactly what I want to do Emmett. It's almost like I have the old Emmett, back you're reading me and knowing what I need but..."

"I know I haven't been the best husband. It's hard to be when you're overseas but I love you, Jenna. I want you to be happy. I'd like to have some kids too."

"That's the thing Emmett. I found out I can't have kids something happened when I lost the baby," Jenna explained, and then began crying.

Emmett took a big breath and made a quick decision to compromise. He loved Jenna, he owed her a life of happiness and he wanted to move forward. This must have been killing Jenna not to be able to tell him. He had to accept this and make her feel better. After all they could always adopt. Couldn't they?

"Jenna I love you; kids, or no kids. Besides we could adopt some day when were ready," Emmett commented, taking Jenna in his arms.

"Oh, Emmett! I do love you."

Emmett began to kiss Jenna. The two of them gave into the passion and soon began making love. Sometime later, satiated in the glow of their passion they smiled at one another and lay arm in arm. They were interrupted by loud knocking on their bedroom door and the door being thrown open.

"Emmett, I went into Paula's room to borrow a sweater, and she's not there." Suzy said as she came in the room.

"Can you give us a moment Suzy," Emmett asked embarrassed, by their nudity.

"Aw, sorry, you two, but this is important," Suzy insisted.

Suzy backed out of the room. Jenna and Emmett quickly dressed. They then went out into the living room where Suzy waited.

"Maybe she's in the bathroom?" Jenna asked.

"No, I checked Jenna," Suzy responded, and then turning to Emmett she said, "I can't find her. You don't think she's with that dweeb Jason?"

"You don't like him either?" Emmett asked.

"No, he's too much like dad," Suzy commented.

"Maybe that is the appeal for Paula," Jenna commented.

"In what way is he like dad?" Emmett asked.

"About six or seven months ago, Paula came home with a black -eye and said she broke-up with Jason. Paula said a door hit her in the eye, but I think he hit her," Suzy explained.

"Why didn't you tell me?" Jenna asked, "I would have talked to her."

"The bastard, I'll kill him," Emmett snarled.

"Don't kill him Emmett. We need you here not in jail; just find Paula, before she does something stupid," Jenna answered.

"Yes, please Emmett," Suzy agreed.

"You don't think they'd elope? Do you?" Emmett asked.

"She's just stupid enough to fall for all his lies, and marry someone just like dad," Suzy answered.

"Where's the phone book I have to check out all the places they can get married in this city."

"Here, Emmett," Jenna replied, handing him the phone book.

Emmett looked through the phone book to find that someone probably Paula had circled three wedding chapels. Two of them were twenty-four hour chapels.

"I think one of these are it. Come on you two let's go." Emmett demanded, as Jenna called a cab.

Emmett only hoped that they wouldn't be too late as he called a cab to take Jenna, Suzy and himself to the first one.

~0~

Chapter 5 - Going to the Chapel

Arriving at the White Wedding Chapel, Emmett went in through the front door followed closely by Jenna and Suzy.

"Please take a seat. I'm sorry a wedding is taking place right now. We can probably marry you in an about an hour," the receptionist sitting at the desk explained.

"Please could you let me know the couple's names? I'm searching for my sister.

"I'm sorry we can't give out names," the receptionist answered.

"Please, my husband is just worried about his pregnant sister. Do you have a Paula Rogers and a Jason Spriet here?" asked Jenna.

"Oh I guess I could tell you then as long as you are not related to the bride and groom. No, the bride and groom are Jabirah Boulos and David Abrams."

"Thank you," Jenna replied pulling Emmett out the front door and to the waiting cab.

"I saved the cab. Hurry up and get in so we can go to the next one Emmett and Jenna," Suzy shouted.

The next chapel didn't yield Paula either. Emmett began to worry they were probably to late when they arrived at the last chapel the Chapel of the Bluebells.

"I have great hopes for this one, Emmett. Paula's favourite flower is a bluebell," Suzy explained.

"Why didn't you say so, we could have gone there sooner," Jenna complained.

"Never mind, we are here now. Let's just go see if Paula is here." Emmett insisted.

The hallway to the chapel was white and adorned with silk roses and bluebells. A lone woman sat at a desk. She was an older woman, probably in her sixties. She had grey hair tucked up in a bun and a flowered dress that hung shapelessly on her.

"Do you want to get married? Because we are all booked up until eleven," the woman said as she saw Emmett and Jenna.

"No, we're looking for my sister's wedding," Emmett stated.

"What are their names?"

"Paula Rogers and Jason Spriet?"

"Oh, the cute redhead with the baby ball out front, and the nice soldier. They got the deluxe ceremony. It should be a lovely wedding you are just in time to see it. If you go quietly in you can probably see the end of it," she answered.

Emmett hurried for the door moving so quickly he beat both Suzy and Jenna to the door by minutes rather than seconds. Jason heard the door open and turned around to stared straight at Emmett.

"Why the hell is he here?" He asked grabbing Paula's arms tightly and spinning her around to face them.

Emmett noted the bruises, even from across the room. It was obvious he done this to Paula.

"I don't know. I didn't tell him Jason," Paula whimpered.

"Lying bitch! You know he hates me," Jason griped and then he hit Paula across the face.

"Keep your hands to yourself you bastard," Emmett yelled.

"Who will stop me? You? The officiate and witnesses have already went into the back to sign my documents, so don't look around for them. It's official dude. She's my wife. You're too late asshole and she does what I say now," Jason needled.

"Jason, don't hurt Paula." Jenna cried. "She's carrying your baby."

"Shut up, Jenna. I love my child. Emmett's a fool to keep you as his wife, I wouldn't. You aren't fit to be near Paula."

"Don't talk to my wife that way," Emmett shouted.

Jason bridged the gap between them and grabbed Jenna's arm. Emmett grabbed Jason by his neck and pulled him away from Jenna.

~0~

Jenna

J enna then grabbed Paula pulling her to safety at the back of the room. Jenna watched in horror as Jason struggled and managed to get free. Jason then struck Emmett in the face with his fists. Emmett had no choice, but to fight back. He couldn't allow him to harm Jenna, Paula, or Suzy, who now stood at the back of the room.

Jenna wanted to leave, but she just couldn't leave Emmett. She knew he had lived through some kind of hell in Afghanistan and fighting Jason couldn't bring back anything, but bad memories back to him. Suzy refused to leave, because she said she had to protect Emmett. Jenna suspected Suzy knew more about Emmett's troubles then she did. Somehow that smarted she was Emmett's wife why couldn't he confide in her. Suzy was so easy to talk to, no wonder Emmett saw fit to tell her and not Jenna. Jenna thought Suzy needed protecting from herself.

Suzy rushed in, as Jenna's granny had said, where angels feared to tread. Her sister-in law Paula had none of the qualities. Emmett and Suzy had she was foolish and head strong. She always did what she wanted until she met Jason. Then all of a sudden she did everything he wanted and her family wishes were irrelevant. Paula had been looking for someone like her dear old daddy, and it seemed she'd found it. Paula refused to leave the room. No matter how many times they both begged her. Suzy held her back as she tried to go to Jason's side.

~0~

Emmett

Emmett felt odd but, he knew he would defeat the insurgent. He wouldn't let him kill Helen. They would get free. God damn!! She shouldn't be here. Why hadn't she come on patrol and been kidnapped? He loved her. But he was a married man. Just thinking about her he felt he cheated on Jenna. He was in love with two women. If they got out of here alive he had to choose. He kept pummeling the insurgent and the man kept fighting back.

"Emmett, please stop you'll kill my husband," Paula's voice came to him. But that was impossible he was in Afghanistan wasn't he?
"Emmett, stop!" Helen begged him.

"Emmett, please stop for me?" begged Suzy.

Emmett looked around and realized where he was. He had
been fighting Jason. It wasn't Helen but Paula that had
spoken to him. His arms fell to his sides and he grew
frightened. He had another episode. He had to get out of
here, before he killed Jason. He turned his back on Jason,
who sat on the floor and went to walk away but Jason raised
his arms and punched Emmett in the back of the head near
his previous injury. Emmett collapsed unconscious on the
floor.

~0~

Chapter 6 - Nightmare

Emmett struggled but the binds on his hands held him tight. There was no way out of this nightmare. He could hear the whimpers of his fellow soldiers in the next room. They were being tortured and his turn was next in line. He wouldn't give up any information, no matter what they did to him. They dragged him into the next room and flung him into a chair strapping him to it by tying his hands and feet.

"You will tell us what we want to know; or the woman will suffer more. So far all we have done is bruised her pretty skin but there is more we can do," his torturer insisted.

Emmett shook his head and refused to say a word. He felt the skin being slowly ripped off his back in small strips with each motion of the whip. His mind tried to think of other things and he thought he almost succeeded when a small gasp of pain escaped his lips. He heard with surprise a peaceful voice say, "There you go. That should help with the pain, Emmett. Rest easy now" and he felt himself drift off to sleep.

He woke again much more alert and looked around to find
the small room he had been in Afghanistan fade away. He
was in a hospital room. Emmett confused and disoriented
wondered if he had been rescued and evacuated to one?
And why had they tied him down? He tried to raise his head
and found it difficult. In fact lifting it made him dizzy. How
had he hurt his head? Oh yes, the bullet that had struck
from the firefight.

"Emmett? Are you awake now?" asked a soft voice, as the
man came in the room. He wore a white coat and appeared
to be a doctor.

"Where am I?" asked Emmett.

"You are in Happy Valley General Hospital. You were in a
fight do you remember?"

Emmett felt confused again and almost asked, "But how did
I get here? I was in Afghanistan.", before he remembered
his escape and what had happened since then. He had come
home to chaos. Paula was pregnant and his father had killed
his mother in a murder suicide. Wait a minute; there was
more to his life then than that. What else had happened?
Why was he in a hospital? He had been searching for Paula
to stop her from marrying Jason. Yes that was correct and
good grief, Paula had married that cretin. If that wasn't bad
enough Emmett had found Jason had bruised her arm and
blackened Paula's eye. At that moment Emmett, had feared
for Paula's life. He had demanded Jason let Paula go. Jason
then threatened Jenna who had grabbed Paula and pulled
her to safety. What had happened next, Emmett didn't quite
remember. Why didn't he remember? Had he done
something horrible? Was that why they tied him down?

Emmett grew frightened and then worried about his sisters and Jenna. Had he done something to them? Or had Jason? He looked around the room. It looked like a normal hospital room not a padded cell. He had a vision in his head of being held in a rubber room. But at least this wasn't one.

"You're with us now Emmett?" the man asked.

"Did I do something wrong?" Emmett ventured to ask motioning to the restraints.

"You were very combative Emmett. You kept insisting we were trying to harm you."

"I'm sorry," Emmett replied feeling stupid was he crazy he didn't remember any of this. Why did this keep happening to him?

"You've been through a lot Emmett."

Emmett didn't answer; he didn't want to talk about it. If he didn't talk about it then it hadn't happened. He wouldn't have to remember the pain and could keep it all compartmentalized somewhere that he wouldn't think about any of what happened, except it kept intruding in his nightmares and then in his daily life when he would slip back in Afghanistan. It was like he was still there. He must have lost his mind. He had slipped back there when he fought Jason, if he hadn't heard Suzy he might have killed Jason. Jason had struck him just above his left ear, right where the bullet had grazed him.

"How long have I been here?"

"A week. You're head injury was severe, Emmett. You need to take greater care for the next little while so that the injury will not reoccur."

"My head was injured?" Emmett asked.

"Yes, you had a prior injury to the same spot. We had to do surgery to remove a blood clot again, but you will be fine provided you take it easy."

"Are my sisters and my wife are okay?" Emmett asked.

"Yes, but they are worried about you. Would you like to see them in a little while?"

"Yes, but could I have these off?" Emmett asked motioning to the restraints.

"As long as you are lucid and remain non-combative. But if you have any more incidents they go back on."

"You're sure I didn't hurt anyone?" Emmett asked horrified.

"No, but it took a number of our staff and a sedative to subdue you."

"I was dreaming, I thought I was in Afghanistan," offered Emmett as an explanation.

"Does that happen a lot?" asked the man removing the restraints.

"You're not just any doctor are you? You're a shrink," Emmett pronounced.

"We prefer to be called psychiatrists but I have a duo specialty, I'm also a board trained neurologist."

"Oh..."

"I'm a Captain in the armed forces. Doctor Pierre Rétrécir," he said introducing himself.

Emmett couldn't help himself he started laughing.

"Yes, a lot of my patients, who can translate French, think it's funny that my last name means shrink. Now that is off your chest, can we talk?"

"About what?" Emmett answered.

"Emmett, let's not play games. You and I both know you suffer from your experiences. It happens to a lot of us."

"Right! Did it happen to you?" Emmett griped.

"Actually it did. I was on a base in Afghanistan that was bombed. Men and women I knew were killed, it really affected me, but talking about it helped."

"I can't talk about this," Emmett stated.

"You have to learn to talk about this Emmett. You can't keep it bottled up inside, or it tries to come bursting out like it's been doing to you."

"I know, but I'm not ready yet," Emmett admitted.

"Okay, how about we talk about this later. I've kept the police away, but they'll want to talk to you too."

"How much trouble am I in with the police?"

"Your sisters and your wife testified that your brother-in-law started the fight. You walked away but not before causing a lot of injuries to Mr. Spriet."

"Is Jason okay?"

"Yes, he was treated for his injuries and released to the military police. He'll be spending the next thirty days in the brig for spousal abuse and the assault on you, before he ships off to Afghanistan next month."

"Will I go to jail and lose my job?"

"No, I spoke to the police and they will drop any charges against you provided you attend sessions with me. Your boss went to bat for you and job will be there in six months provided you pass your psyche evaluation. "

"Do you think I'm crazy?" Emmett griped.

"No, I think you've been through hell and need to talk about it. You talked with a doctor briefly in Afghanistan but you didn't tell them all that happened to you did you?" the doctor asked shrewdly.

"How did you know that? I thought you worked at this hospital?"

"Yes, actually I do, but your commanding officer asked for me when you were brought in."

"How would Captain Campbell know I was here?" Emmett asked surprised.

"Your sister Susan called him when you were brought in. He's been here for the last week. He's waiting to see you too, but I advised him that I would let him know when I thought you were ready to see him."

"Can I see my sisters and my wife Jenna and then the Cap?" Emmett asked.

"If we can make a deal! You promise to tell me one thing today, that happened to you in Afghanistan and I'll let you visit for a few minutes."

"Am I a prisoner?"

"No, Emmett. You're a patient, one that I'd like to help if you'll let me," Doctor Rétrécir replied softly.

"Fine, we were on patrol in Afghanistan when some insurgents kidnapped us." Emmett answered, reluctantly.

"That's a start Emmett. We'll talk some more, much later in group. For now I'll get your family."

Group? Was the man crazy Emmett wasn't about to tell a bunch of strangers, about his experiences. He could barely get those words past his lips. How would he talk about any of this?

A few minutes later the door opened and Jenna walked in by herself. She had a fake smile plastered on her face, like she thought Emmett would break at any moment.

"The doctor said I could come in first. Why didn't you tell me about this Emmett? Never mind I know why you didn't. We put so much stress on you when you come home expecting you to fix all our problems. You've been amazing, but now it's time to help you Emmett," Jenna exclaimed.

"Did I scare you?" Emmett asked noticing that she didn't come closer.

"Maybe a little, you know how my dad used to flip out at the least little thing."

"I'm sorry Jenna."

"No, I'm sorry. I should have known you can't come back from battle unscarred. But you didn't even tell me you were injured over there." Jenna complained, "Suzy had to tell me. How did she know and I didn't?"

"Suzy only knows what they told her on the phone. She pretended to be you, when they called," Emmett explained.

"Will you tell me what happened to you Emmett?" Jenna begged.

"I can't yet; but I will when I can," Emmett promised.

"Fine, don't share with me, but at least tell your doctor."

"I promise I'll tell you when I can." Emmett insisted.

"That will have to do. I spoke to the lawyer our guardianship for Suzy went down before this so you don't have to worry. Suzy and Paula want to see you. I'll let them in," Jenna stated.

Suzy followed with the same fake smile on her face. Paula followed behind her. She glared at Emmett like he was the scum of the earth. What was her problem, he wondered? Had he done something to her? Then he remembered what the doctor had said about Jason. She obviously still cared about the asshole. How would he keep her away from him? Maybe his tour in Afghanistan would make Jason straighten out.

Suzy looked at Emmett again like he would break. He should have said something when they came in now it looked like he had lost his chance. Suzy probably thought he was crazy. Damn it! Emmett should be able to protect his family. He felt emasculated. He was supposed to protect his family and instead Jason had gotten the jump on him and he had acted like he was still in Afghanistan it had obviously scared them.

"Hi, long time, no see," Emmett said breaking the ice.

"Oh, Emmett I'm so glad you're okay," Suzy replied jumping in his arms.

"Don't look at me, to come and hug you. I just wanted to tell you how much I hate you. Because of you my sweet husband will go to Afghanistan sooner. He won't even be here when our baby is born," whined Paula.

"I don't schedule tours of duty. You're making no sense," Emmett responded.

"He fought a decorated hero a superior soldier you think they don't hold that against Jason. You just had to wreck everything. I wish you'd died over there."

Emmett felt like rolling up in a ball and doing just that he loved his sister and she was right he'd wrecked things for Jason. The guy was a schmuck, Paula loved him. He should have handled things better.

"Shut-up Paula. You heard the doctor," Suzy cautioned.

"No, Emmett needs to know what he did;" Paula continued, "Just because he went to Afghanistan doesn't mean he can act like this."

"You stupid bitch. Your sweet husband abused you. He punched you in the eye and he hit you as well as twisted your arm. What should Emmett have done let Jason continue harming you maybe even kill your baby?" Suzy yelled.

"He wouldn't have harmed us," Paula insisted.

"You're delusional," Suzy insisted.

Emmett's head began to hurt and at that moment, he just wished they'd all leave. He felt angry and he wanted to hit someone.

"Go!" he commanded.

"What did you say?" asked Jenna shocked.

"I'm sorry. My headaches, can you come back later Please?" Emmett apologized.

"We're sorry Emmett. We'll come back later right Jenna and Paula?" Suzy chimed in.

"Yes, I will," agreed Jenna.

"Fine, but this discussion isn't over Emmett. I have to see if they'll let me visit Jason anyway."

"Jenna?"

"Yes, Emmett?"

"Look after my sisters. Please?" Emmett requested.

"I will don't worry, Emmett. Just get better." Jenna said kissing Emmett.

Emmett watched as they left and felt guilty that he was relieved to see them go. Still he was worried about Paula. He hoped they wouldn't let her see Jason and that she realize just how badly Jason had treated her and divorce him. Emmett just wanted to curl up in a ball and shut them all out he was tired, oh so tired of all their problems but he couldn't do that he had to somehow find a way to pull himself together because they needed him.

~0~

Chapter 7 - Return to Hell

Emmett woke up and looked beside his bed. He could see the faint rays of the morning sun coming in the room. His foot reached out and prodded the arm he saw. He wasn't seeing things Captain Campbell sat in a chair there.

"Captain," Emmett cried sitting up in his bed.

"At ease Emmett," Captain Campbell replied.

"Have you been here since last night Captain?"

"Yes, you snore boy."

"I do?"

"Okay, you make soft girly noises, when you sleep," Captain Campbell kidded.

"Well gee, thanks Captain, for letting me know that."

"I heard you too had some flashbacks to our time in Afghanistan."

"Too?"

"Yes, we didn't come off easy from that skirmish did we?"

"No, but I'm fine."

"No, you're not Emmett and you won't be until you can talk about what happened to us. What happened to you! I found it hard to talk to the shrink, but once I started talking about what happened it got better."

"I can't talk about it captain. How can anyone else even understand?"

"I was there. Try talking to me first. Tell me what you remember. I'll start the conversation. Cadet Tommy Harrow disappeared on regular patrol and some villagers said he'd dishonoured Raishma Wahidi .Searching we found Raishma Wahidi dead, but no evidence of Tommy. Where did we go from there Emmett?"

"We asked the villagers where they could have taken him, but were surrounded by the Taliban sympathizers and taken for questioning," Emmett answered.

"Then tell me what happened after we were all taken prisoner."

"They started torturing us, for three long days," Emmett responded.

"Three days Emmett? Are you sure it was three days?"

"That's what I remember."

"You're deceiving yourself," Captain Campbell stated.

"You have to remember to heal."

"I don't understand, we were there three days," Emmett claimed.

"What happened the first day?"

"They tied us up beat us and threw us in a room."

"On the second day?"

"It was hard to tell what day it was."

"Emmett, tell me."

"They demanded to know information about troop movements and plans."

"And did you tell them anything?"

"You know I didn't, Captain."

"What did they do to us to get the information?"

"I didn't see it I don't know what they did to the squad."

"Emmett, close your eyes and place yourself there. What do you see?"

"I'm in a room, it's dingy but there are powerful lights in my eyes."

"Who is in the room look around and tell me."

"Cadet Tommy Harrow, Lieutenant Fred Aswad, Cadet Helen Bowman and Cadet Paul Mancini and you sir, are all in the room. You are all tied to chairs."

"And?"

"Some men hit us. But we didn't tell them anything."

"Then what happened?" asked the captain.

"They took us back to another room after I passed out from the beatings."
"That's not what occurred, Emmett."

"Go back to the room in your mind."

"No!" Emmett replied, clenching his jaw.

"Emmett, you can't heal unless you allow yourself to remember and your sisters need you whole."

"Fine, then they hurt Helen."

"Yes, they hurt Helen, tortured her and then they killed her...right in front of us," Captain Campbell responded, as if he choked.

Emmett closed his eyes trying to shutout the memory, but now that Captain Campbell had reminded him, the memory played in front of his eyes. He hadn't been able to save Helen. Captain Campbell's eyes met his in recognition of their shared pain.

"None of us could save her Emmett. We've got to quit blaming ourselves."

Emmett thought about what had happened next. Their captors had thought torturing and killing Helen would break them all, but it had just made the squad angrier. Their captors became wrathful when the squad refused to say any words at all, and began whipping them and tearing strips of flesh from their backs. This had gone on for a week. Emmett had known the time, because he could see sunlight and moonlight coming in the room. How had he forgotten that they had done this too him for a week?

Emmett remembered on the seven day finally getting free, by twisting his wrist and tearing bits of skin off his wrists; as he shed the manacles they used to restrain him. Emmett had killing his main tormenter before he could raise the call to the others. He had then used metal from the chair to free the others. Then they had escaped and Emmett had gotten most of them to the base and to hospital.

"You didn't see us again," the captain said. "What a reward, after you had done your best to save your squad."

"I didn't save you all," Emmett answered quietly.

"You aren't God, Emmett. You did what most men could not. You rescued us, Tommy, Fred, Pete and me."

"Fred and Pete died."

"That wasn't something you could control. How many others could drive with a bullet wound to the head .You had a collapsed lung and a severed artery in your leg and yet you managed to get us to the base. You are hero man."

"I don't feel like a hero."

"Then you're pretty stupid Second Lieutenant Rogers, sir," Tommy commented from the door.

"Tommy? I'm seeing things?"

"Nope, pretty good imitations aren't they?" Tommy asked tapping his artificial legs.

"You're really here?"

"Of course, you saved my life. I heard from you could use a visit."

Emmett wiped tears from his eyes and then felt embarrassed.

"Got some dust in my eyes," he said.

"Me too, Emmett," Tommy responded. "Hey, you got another chair there?"

"Sure Tommy. Right there," Emmett said.

"Emmett I've been talking to a shrink for a while now. I know how much of this was my fault. If I hadn't ...no, I won't go there anymore. Things happen and we deal with them. We make mistakes and move on. We have to realize we can't save everyone," Tommy said like a mantra. "Emmett you saved my life and I'll always be grateful to you. And it sounds like you came home to your own little hell. Your mom and dad die and leave you to raise your sisters? Understand the oldest one is knocked-up with some abuser's kid you want me and the Captain to straighten the jerk out?"

"No, thanks Tommy, that's what got me here, besides my sister barely, speaks to me now."

"No, what got you here was me, Emmett. I got you injured in Afghanistan. I was the one who wandered into a trap and you all came to rescue me."

"It wasn't your fault Tommy. The insurgents wanted to kidnap us they would found a way.

"Thank you, Emmett. Now quit blaming yourself over something we had no control over. I may have lost my legs but I have my life thanks to you. I met a nurse Leanna and we're getting married. How about that? The bachelor finds true love. I'd liked it if you be my best man. The captain has already said he's coming."

"Congratulations, Tommy,"

"Then you'll do it? You'll be my best man?"

"Are you sure you want me?" asked Emmett.

"I couldn't think of anyone better and neither could Leanna when I told her how you saved me."

"Can I bring my wife, Jenna and my sisters? That is if Paula will talk to me."

"Of course you can Emmett. You were always fair to me. You and the captain and I didn't always listen. Your sister will come around too."

"So when do you head home to Winnipeg, Tommy?"

"Trying to get rid of me, Emmett? Because I have a week's vacation and I'm sticking around till you get tired of us."

"Thanks guys." Emmett responded.

"Hey, what's good on the television?" Tommy asked flicking it on. "Soccer?"

Emmett felt happier watching the soccer game than he had been since he'd come home. He knew he had work ahead of him and life would never be easy, but he could handle life. He just had to think positively and talk to the shrink, and then he could go home and help his sisters. He could do this.

"Where did Captain Campbell go?" Emmett asked, suddenly not seeing him.

"Emmett, buddy I'm sorry this is my fault. I got the captain killed. You tried to save him; but in the end he died."

"What?"

"He's dead Emmett; he died before we even got back to the base. You don't remember?"

"I don't remember."

"Yes, you do. You don't want to; but deep in your subconscious you do."

"He was injured the Knife had him; but he survived I got him to help in time."

"No, Emmett he died in the truck. He bled out."

"But that's impossible. I saw him here."

"I saw things too, Emmett. Until you can talk about what happened over there, it's going to happen a lot."

"What is going to happen a lot?" Emmett responded avoiding the obvious.

"Seeing things that aren't really happening… I'm having flashbacks of Afghanistan."

"Captain Campbell's really dead?"

"Yes, the man's dead. I went to his grave. I had to; I had to pay my tribute to get on with my life. If my shrink hadn't seen me through this I'd be in the same shape you're in buddy."

"How did he die?"

"*The Knife,* man. He stripped too many pieces of flesh and the captain bled and bled. We tried to stem the flow but he died in the truck."

"I don't remember."

"You will. You're mind's trying to protect you but you got to open up to your doc. He's a good one."

"Thanks Tommy I'll try. Will you come back?"

"I'll be back pal. You hang in there."

Emmett shut his eyes and tried to sleep. He'd fight this he had to remember but not now right now he wanted to sleep. Within a few minutes he'd drifted off.

~0~

Chapter 8 - Getting Better

D octor Rétrécir began his therapy sessions with questions lots of questions. Ones that Emmett at first felt reluctant to answer. He wanted to open up and admit what happened in Afghanistan but the words were hard to come by. Emmett began talking about small events and then the bigger events. He still seemed to have no active memory of Captain Campbell's death and that worried him. He tried to admit that to Doctor Rétrécir; but the declaration stuck in his throat like food trapped. The medicines he took for his depression at first made him feel oddly out of touch but after adjustments he was feeling better , happier if only for a few moments.

Time went by and he was mystified that his sisters were still willing to put up with him. Thank goodness for Jenna who had stepped up and taken guardianship of Suzy. She'd also taken Paula under her wing and was sharing the family home with them.

Suzy hadn't meant to tell him but she revealed that Paula had fought back saying that she alone had more right to the family home then Jenna. Jenna insisted as Emmett's wife that she protected the family. She was a Rogers and she loved them. Jenna would love them no matter what they did to her if only for herself and Emmett. Paula had grudgingly given Jenna respect and tolerated her in the house but she was still riding Jenna every chance she got. Suzy thought she was missing Jason and mad at Emmett and taking it out on Paula. Emmett tried to get Paula to speak to him, but she refused to talk.

Emmett did talk to Doctor Rétrécir about his sisters and his relationship with his wife. Talking about Jenna made him open up the floodgates of Afghanistan. He started chatting about and how Officer Cadet Helen Bowman had bonded and how they had made plans to be together.

"You feel guilty about breaking your vows and feeling human in a war zone?"

"Yes, I should have stepped away and remembered I was married."

"You made vows; but you had distanced yourself from Jenna and from the problems you had here."

"Are we talking about my stint as a soldier or as a husband?"

"Both. Why do you believe you signed up to fight?"

"Because I had to save my children...I mean my country from the Taliban and all those people that planned the world trade center bombing."

That's telling don't you think Emmett?"

"In what way?"

You mentioned your children but you have no children. Were those the only reasons Emmett? Didn't you also want to escape your father and all the responsibilities that fell on your young head? I speak of the sisters who were like your children and the girlfriend who placed more responsibility by becoming pregnant and then losing your child."

"What are you talking about? They are my sisters and I had a duty to Jenna. I got her pregnant."

"Yes, you were a young virile young man who didn't take precautions."

"I did take precautions they didn't work."

That's right you were being responsible and fate intervened and then you lost that child."

"What has all this to do with what happened to me over in Afghanistan and what happened since I came back?"

""Emmett, you were just beginning to open up. Don't you think you should be honest with yourself? You've had trial after trial in your life. You lost your child and you felt powerless like you felt all your life."

"I don't feel powerless!!'Emmett insisted.

"Don't you? Haven't you since you were a small child and especially after Dianna disappeared."

"I won't speak of Dianna," Emmett insisted.

"Isn't it true that your father chased her away from your home because she was pregnant?"

"I won't speak of Dianna," Emmett said again more firmly. "Fine, then why don't we speak of the true trial burden in your life? Admit that your father was an abuser who covered his own securities with drugs and alcoholic and your mother enabled him."

"How did you know that?"

"Emmett you just confirmed what I suspected."

"My mother wasn't an enabler. She was cowed by him... abused by him. She loved him more than her own life."

"So much so that she allowed him to kill her."

"She needed protecting and I wasn't there to protect her. I should have been there," Emmett shouted

"People make their own choices, Emmett. Some good some bad; but what we do affects others. Your mother was dying she knew she was dying. So was your father. He decided to take the easiest road in his mind and kill both of them."

"I should have protected her. If only I had stayed at the house and not made waves with him..."

"You have a hero complex, Emmett. You think you should be able to save everyone but it's not always possible you're not God. It's something you'll have to work on. You couldn't have saved your mother any more than you could have saved the men who died in Afghanistan."

Emmett had broken down then and cried to his shame. But he found the talking grew easier and soon he was sharing his experiences in Afghanistan with Doctor Rétrécir and he felt drained. Days went by and he began to get better with Doctor Rétrécir's help he was beginning to deal with his post-traumatic stress disorder. The doctor had emphasized that certain thoughts about his trauma caused stress and made his symptoms worse. Identify thoughts about the world and himself that made him feel afraid or upset. With the help of your Doctor Rétrécir, he learned to replace these thoughts with more accurate and less distressing thoughts. he also had to learn to cope with feelings of anger, guilt, and fear and realize that the traumatic events he lived through were not his fault and that he could do nothing to change the past.

Doctor Rétrécir would tap and he would focus on that and not the memories that triggered his PTSD. Emmett began using the therapy to contain the memories that threatened to overwhelm him. Soon Emmett was able to share in group with other soldiers. He began to learn more and more how to cope and he promised to see his new therapist weekly after he was let go from the hospital.

He felt stronger, much stronger than he ever had before as he left the hospital and got into the car next to Jenna. They had a lot of work to do but he vowed he patch up his marriage back together and the two of them would raise Suzy to adulthood. up He also look after Paula and her baby until her husband came home from Afghanistan hopefully but that time he would have grown into a husband worthy of Paula
They would all be okay for he was going home at last.

~0~

Chapter 9 - Epilogue

A lot had happened since Emmett had returned from Afghanistan. Emmett had sought help for his post-traumatic stress disorder and with help from family and friends, now had it under control and had gone on to start his job as a policeman at the Happy Valley Police Department. Paula had given birth to a nine pound boy she named Gregory Emmett Spriet.

Emmett looked over at his sisters. They looked so happy. He noted how their eyes followed Greg (Paula's seven year old son), as he played with his radio controlled Air Hogs. Christmas had been wonderful despite the two empty chairs. How he missed Jenna. He had been so blindsided by the divorce papers she wanted him to sign two years ago. Somehow he thought she would change her mind.

Jenna had been working shift work as a nurse which always seemed to go against his shifts as a police officer. Because of this he should have known how unhappy she had become, but instead Emmett had happily accepted the rewards of his blossoming career. He had advanced to Detective Sergeant and now investigated a lot of the top crimes like assaults and murder. His partner Detective Sergeant Cameron Grenor tried to warn him he spread himself thin, but Emmett foolishly didn't listen~ until he walked in on Cameron and Jenna in bed. Emmett was gobsmacked. Cameron had called in sick, and instead he cheated with Emmett's wife?

Emmett couldn't believe she would do such a thing especially when Paula and Greg, or even Suzy, could have walked in on her in bed with Cameron. He had wanted to yell and scream and shout, instead he'd gone to his therapist's office and vented. When he'd come home Jenna had left. She'd moved in with Cameron. To say his working relationship was tenuous was an understatement. He didn't trust the man who was his partner, Cameron and Emmett only exchanged single words and only when obviously necessary. He had waited impatiently for the divorce papers and they arrived, one morning just before work.

Emmett had glanced over them and signed them planning on taking them over to Jenna after work, unfortunately his day got longer when Cameron called in sick. Emmett had put in a full day with all the paperwork and finished at ten in the evening~ too late to see Jenna. Emmett had gone home only to find Jenna there crying. His two sisters were crying too. He knew something bad had happened.

"Is it Jason?" Emmett had asked.

"No, Jason is fine. Jenna needs to talk to you," Paula had answered. "I'll talk to you later, Emmett."

Then Paula had quietly left.

"I don't understand. Tell me what has happened."

"Cameron left me. When he found out, he's gone to London, Ontario. He won't be your partner anymore, you'll be happy to know," Jenna answered and then began crying.

"I'm sorry Jenna. I know you cared about him."

"Oh, Emmett, you were always too nice for your own good. I left you for another man and you tell me you're sorry for me? I'm such a terrible person. I was never enough for you.""

"Jenna, you know and I know it wasn't only your fault that we broke up..."

"I'm sorry Emmett. I made a huge mistake Every time I turn around I hurt you." Jenna said interrupting.

Emmett hadn't known what to say. Suddenly she wanted him back but only after she'd been dumped. is pride wouldn't let him say anything, but then he started thinking about all the times she had supported him and how she had helped him through his post-traumatic stress disorder. Shouldn't he be the bigger person and reach out? Put those hurt feelings aside at least to comfort Jenna?

Jenna started crying louder and Emmett surprised himself by saying "Maybe we can go to couple's counselling and try again."
"I don't know if you'll really want to when you hear what I have to say Emmett, You see I've got breast cancer Emmett. It's very advanced," Jenna had stated bluntly between the tears.

Emmett's heart had dropped into his mouth and he felt a deep pain in his stomach, when he had heard this news. He realized despite all the hurt and bad feelings between them, he still loved Jenna. How could Jenna have cancer? Emmett and Jenna talked long into the night and hashed out some feelings. Emmett then convinced Jenna to stay the night and then the next night. Jenna soon moved back in and they resumed their marriage, this time actually working at it. As Jenna fought back against the cancer, Emmett felt like he had fallen in love with her all over again. Jenna too insisted she felt the same.

As time seem to fly by with cancer treatments and appointments Emmett found he had been assigned a new partner Detective Sergeant Brad Owens. At first he thought Brad would be a great partner but Brad Owens was a hot-dogger who always wanted the limelight and the credit. He constantly and creatively slanted things his way to make Emmett look bad and Brad look good. All the time Emmett took off to help Jenna, being used against Emmett as well. Emmett got fed up and complained that he wanted a new partner and they retaliated by partnering him with no one. Emmett at first was insulted then realized it was better that way especially when he had to take time off to be with Jenna.

Jenna seemed to rally and Emmett had been sure her doctor's appointment would tell them she had beaten the cancer, earlier this year. However, that was not to be as the doctor told her the cancer had spread to her brain and lungs. In May this year, Emmett was there to hold her hand and speak to her as she drifted in and out of consciousness. He heard her say as she seemed on the verge of passing. "I'm so glad he'll be happy again." and then she turned as if she saw him and said" I love you Emmett. Be happy again."

Emmett had been devastated but his sisters had seen him through it all. Lord knows they had been there to help Nurse Jenna, and take care of her. Suzy had done all that even as she trained to be a police officer. Emmett wasn't sure how he felt about Suzy being a cop too, but he knew was proud of her. Suzy had graduated top of her class and would start at the Happy Valley police station early in the New Year.

He would miss both his sisters, now that Suzy would get her own apartment and Paula moved to London, Ontario, to live with Jason. Paula told Emmett only last week that Jason's tour overseas ended January 17 and he had known what that meant to his happy existence with his sisters and nephew. Tomorrow both his sisters would leave home.

Emmett wanted to convince Paula not to live with Jason. He still didn't trust him not to hit her, but Paula insisted Jason had changed and he would never lay a hand on either her or Greg. Emmett had taken Jason aside and talked with him the last time he'd come home, promising to put him in the ground if he hurt Paula like he had, when she was pregnant. Jason apologized citing immaturity and Emmett almost believed him, especially when he started talking about how he wanted his son Greg to look up to him. But then Jason had spoiled it all by yelling at Paula. Only the fact that Jason had signed up for another tour starting in March, stopped Emmett from telling Paula she was mistaken. After all Paula was a grown woman of twenty five. He couldn't dictate to her. She had to find her own way as much as he hated that.

Tomorrow was New Year's Day. The last decade had its highs but an awful lot of lows. This had to be a better year. Emmett counted on it and he knew that if he focused on his career that was the way to go. After all he was a lead investigator, one day maybe he'd be the chief of police. A man should dream big. That's what Jenna always said. Emmett wanted to remember her and make those dreams come true.

Emmett looked back at his sisters, they would be okay. Susan and Paula had grown into strong woman, and if they needed him they knew his door was always open. He had a nephew, Greg, who looked up to him. The pain of loss would fade. Susan wanted to introduce him to a teacher she knew, maybe he'd take her up on it. He could do that maybe... He didn't have to marry her, just go on a date.

Life would get better as long as you have family and Emmett knew he had that in spades. His sisters and his nephew whether near, or far, loved him. He had a career that he loved. He was blessed. He just had to believe that and move forward. Who knew what the future held?

Looking back he thought it could get any worse, so maybe just maybe this year would be better. Hello New Year, I'm ready he thought.

THE END or is it? Read on ~

Emmett investigates the work of a serial killer in~ A Penny Saved A Murder Earned-Book 1 of The Kelly Murder Mysteries an excerpt is on the next page or buy e-books and paperbacks available at Amazon~ Book 2 of The Kelly Murder Mysteries the death of a choir teacher in~ A Diller a Dollar a Really Dead Scholar and Book 3 of The Kelly Murder Mysteries~ a tourist in~ Betty Blue Lost Her Holiday Shoe, or Book 4 of The Kelly Murder Mysteries~ the killer of the mayor and a married couple close to the Kelly's in What Will Poor Robin Do?

Also find an excerpt from Stray Bullet- Expected Release date June 2017

A new sheriff finds his new officers murdered and must investigate why they died and whether the new drug scourge fentanyl is behind it.

Also find and excerpt from Dreams Can Kill Amnesiac Sharon Alexander must strive to remember before force against her strike again only this time succeeding in killing her.

Thank you for reading this story. If you have enjoyed these stories, please think about leaving me a few words of review at your favourite retailer.
Sincerely S. G. Lee

Excerpt from A Penny Saved A Murder Earned ~Chapter 1 - Bloody Shoes

"A penny saved is a penny earned" ~ Benjamin Franklin

T he blood streaked across the floor, but he had carefully sidestepped it. Stupid bitch! She got what she deserved. How dare she defile his Angel's property? He hadn't left a trace...had he? No, he was too clever by half.

A voice he didn't recognize interrupted his thoughts, "I didn't spot you entering. Working late, dear? Of course, I forgot; you have an early opening tomorrow."

The man strode closer to the killer and the body lying on the floor, "Wait a minute, you aren't the lady. Who are you? You shouldn't be here," the man continued clearly alarmed.

"You shouldn't be here either," the murderer insisted.

"You, you killed Megan. I'm telling."

"Really? You know this was something you shouldn't be allowed to see."

"I'm leaving. I didn't notice anything," the man lied, witnessing the blood.

"I'm sorry pal. Wrong place, wrong time!" the killer answered.

The homeless man ran dodging racks, finally deciding to hide behind some shelving. The killer ran after him, puzzled for a moment because he could see no trace of the homeless person. The murderer then laughed, as he realized how foolish the vagrant was being, his stench gave him away. He subdued the man with a Taser gun. Waiting seconds he then pulled the man from his hiding place. Taking ties from within his pocket; he fastened the man's arms and feet. Satisfied that the homeless person was now trussed up like a turkey, he smiled.

"P...P....P...Please! I don't want to die!" the man cried, visibly sweating and starting to shake.

The man tried to kick out his legs and arms but failed.

"You've heard about fate? Well sorry but this is your fate, buddy!" the murderer explained.

"P...P...P...Please, I'm begging you! Couldn't you let me go? I won't tell! I'll move to another city. Besides who would listen to a homeless man?"

"Someone would. My Angel would."

The homeless man then smiled as if to gain trust from this killer, "You won't hurt the lady who owns the store, will you?" he asked.

"I would never harm my Angel. How dare you?" the killer responded outraged.

"S...S...S...Sorry! I didn't mean to insult you! Please just let me go. I'm harmless ask anyone...."

"What is your name?"

"Why do you need my name?" He asked looking puzzled then reconsidering he answered, "My name is Al."

The killer put his gloves back on and smoothed them and then turned his back on his victim.

"You're going to kill me now. Aren't you? Just don't harm the sweet lady who owns this store. Will it hurt?" the man asked resigned.

"I would never hurt my Angel. She is sweet isn't she? Unfortunately that also makes unscrupulous people take advantage of her."

"I promise I would never take advantage of her kindness. I wouldn't!!! She's the best part of my day and this city, Happy Valley, Ontario. She picked me up from the gutter and helped me."

"I know you wouldn't and it hurts me to do this. Tell you what though, I'll make your death painless because I like you, Al," the killer offered, feeling suddenly sorry for the man.

Then he checked himself. Living on the streets was hell; maybe he was doing the guy a favour? Yes, of course he was. Taking a pill bottle out of his pocket and opening the dispenser, he placed some in a coffee cup he took from the sideboard. He filled the cup with the tepid coffee from the coffee pot, stirring the pills in rapidly.

"C...c...c...couldn't you let me go? I won't tell and I'll watch over her when you're not here."
"Sorry, times up, Al. Here now, drink this coffee," the assassin commanded placing the mug at Al's lips.

Al tried not to drink and spit some of the coffee out, but the assassin plugged his nose and the cup was soon empty.

"Admit it Al, you had a crappy life. Just give in and go to the light. I hear good things wait there for people like you," the killer stated.

Al tried to fight some more, but he soon found it was losing battle. Al's breathing slowed as he slipped into a deep sleep and stopped breathing altogether. His age and living on the streets made the pills work fast.

Now what to do with the body? The killer thought. His Angel must not find this man's remains here, bad enough he left Megan's body here for his Angel to find. He couldn't hide Megan though she needed to be found. Every needed to know she suffered for her crime. Maybe even his Angel would see Megan's evil and protect herself from people like that. This man, Al however knew his Angel and she cared about him. It was so like her to look after the homeless. He could let her cry over Al. Where could he put the man so he wouldn't be found?

The dumpster of course...the perfect place for Al! The day after tomorrow was garbage day. Covered in garbage no one would find Al.

~0~

The next day
Lily

Ominous clouds replaced the morning's sunlight

turning the skies to shades of deep purple and navy blue, streaked with gray. Lily Kelly stared at the sky for moment, and then departed the courthouse doors in Happy Valley, Ontario, Canada, skipping down the steps. The city looked its age of over a hundred as the buildings downtown looked old and decrepit. If only the town could find some money to fix downtown Lily thought.

Then her mind turned to Amelia, her cousin and best friend. Amelia needed Lily to support her in her grief. Lily had a fight with her husband Horace again this morning about how much time he was spending at the office and how much time she spent supporting Amelia. Lily was always working, and so was Horace, so how much time was Rose their fourteen year old daughter really getting?

Lily had won in court, but all she could think about was her family. Everyone needed her and she felt like she was being pulled in three different directions. Something had to give and it looked like it was her job. She would have to cut back on some of her work. Her family had to come first.

Lily stumbled some more over the steps only stopping from hurrying across the courtyard to her office, when her heel broke on her shoe. Today was supposed to be about her victory after her win in court; but it appeared with her expensive shoe's heel breaking, she was mistaken. They ought to get the ruts in the paving stones fixed; that was her reflection as she cursed her bad break. What did they say about omens? Maybe she should have taken a hint from the heavens' darkening? She noted as her bad luck had seemed to get worse with the arrival of some reporters.

"Ms. Kelly, give us a statement about the Rockwood case?" yelled one reporter.

"Ms. Kelly, how does the Sulimani family feel about your victory?" yelled another.

One bold reporter stepped forward, "Crown Attorney Kelly, congratulations on your win. Was it hard to try a case which involved a council member?" asked Paul Knight from the local television station, thrusting a microphone in Lily's face.

"Anyone who commits a crime in Happy Valley will be tried by the Crown with the full force of the law, despite their office. So no, I did not find it difficult to do my job," Lily replied testily.

"Thank you, Ms. Kelly. What does the Sulimani family think about the judgement?"

"Amani Sulimani was five years old, when Zebadiah Rockwood's truck went through a red light. His truck struck the back of the Sulimani's SUV killing her. He then left the scene pursued by good Samaritans, who wished to stop Mr. Rockwood from continuing driving drunk: a pursuit caused by Mr. Rockwood's actions, which put a number of lives in danger."

"Will the family be comforted with this conviction?" queried another reporter.

"Amani Sulimani existed as their only child. Mr. Rockwood's conviction will not bring her back, but hopefully will bring some peace of mind to her family knowing he will be behind bars." Lily answered.

"Do you sense, given your own personal tragedies that you'll be able to get a sentence fitting the crime?"

"My family's history does not come into my trial cases, only the person's guilt."

"And when will sentencing take place?" asked another reporter.

"Sentencing will take place next month."

"Thank you Ms. Kelly. This is Paul Knight reporting, with an update on the Zebadiah Rockwood's drunken driving case. Zebadiah Rockwood was a long time council member here in Happy Valley. He took a leave of absence to deal with his legal issues. Mr. Rockwood was charged with impaired driving causing death, two counts of failing to remain at the scene of an accident and dangerous driving last December. When asked about the conviction today Mr. Rockwood and his lawyer issued a no comment. We will have the complete story for you at six pm. Paul Knight reporting for CHPV-TV."

Lily hated speaking on camera, even though it was part of her job as the Crown attorney, so she was glad the scrum had been completed.

She hated sounding tough and unyielding but it was all in the description of her job title. She had fought difficult challenges to get this job and she had to work hard and fight hard to keep it. After all there were aspects of her job her she loved like putting the bad people that would harm others away. The press was gone and she was now free to go to her office to file her reports and leave early. She crossed the street, entered her building and went straight up to her office.

"Victory is mine!" Lily Kelly cried triumphantly as she walked into her office.

"So you won?" asked Colleen Finn, her administrative assistant.

"Yes, I bested that idiot, Michael Taylor. He thought he would beat me in court. He actually believed his client would win."

"Good for you, boss, I knew you would nail his lily white ass to the wall. He's such a scumbag lawyer all his clients seem to be as guilty as hell."

"Colleen! Language! But thank-you," Lily answered, showing pearly white teeth.

Colleen looked expectantly at Lily and she felt stupid did she miss something? Oh the joke! Lily hadn't laughed at Colleen's wit.

"Funny, I got it. Zebadiah Rockwood's sentencing takes place next month, but he will be held until then; no bail, no goodbyes to his favourite watering hole. As the Crown, I'll recommend the longest sentence I can get that he can serve. It's victories like these which make my job worthwhile. I don't know how much satisfaction this will give that little girl's family, but at least they'll know her killer remains in jail. He can't take another life again, because he will be incarcerated."

Lily went over to her desk and sat down.

"Can you imagine Michael Taylor, tried to use the defence that Rockwood was not drunk. Just tired? He claimed Rockwood drank only after the accident, while driving his company's truck; so the company couldn't possibly be responsible,"

"I believe you told me that before," Colleen commented, "However I'm glad you proved he'd drank so much before getting in the truck. That proved he was legally under the influence when the accident occurred. I hope I was some help in that aspect."

"Yes, you were invaluable."

"Thanks, Lily."

"It's still early; only nine forty-five, and my day's clear until what, two-thirty?"

"That's correct." Colleen replied.

Colleen checked a day planner, frowning, "Is everything okay, Lily? You seem a little down."

"Everything is fine. Amelia's grand opening starts at noon, but I promised to be there sooner if possible. If I go right now, I'll surprise her," Lily grabbed her coat to leave.

"I'm glad she's doing so well. Although after what happened, Amelia needs the encouragement. Please tell her, I'll try to get to her store another day. I hope her store has great success."

"Thank-you, I will tell Amelia. Hold all my calls Colleen. Unless it's urgent then call my cell."

"I'll do that. What time should I say you'll be back?" Colleen responded to a departing Lily.

"Tell whoever asks that I'll be back after two p.m..."

"And if they ask where you are?" Colleen questioned.

"Tell them I'm meeting with a witness," Lily replied with a wink.

"If there's cake bring me back a piece. Please, boss?" Colleen begged.

"I ordered a cake, but it's not supposed to arrive until one thirty so we'll see. I'm leaving now. Remember only urgent calls to my cell phone." Lily cautioned, leaving through the front door.

She twisted her shimmering brown hair back up into its traditional bun. Pulling out her cell phone, she dialled Amelia's store. There was no answer. How odd! Amelia must be busy putting out last minute stock.

~0~

A few minutes ago

A lone male walked into the store. His left hand held a gun while his right hand steadied it. He strode in with caution. His dark brown eyes dart from corner to corner, searching for an assailant. His well over six-foot tall frame slouched. Ruggedly handsome, with dark brown hair clipped short to his head; he was dressed in a dark blue jacket and dress pants; a badge is also clipped to his belt buckle. Finding the scene secure he putting his gun away and pulled a pair of gloves out of his suit coat pocket and a pair of booties, which he slipped on his shoes.

He checked the victim. No pulse. Advancing forward, he bent down to check the second woman; her phone still in her hand, her head bloody. He noted the second victim was still breathing, though unconscious. He looked around, as if waiting for someone. Deciding they weren't coming yet, he took out a mini recorder. He started scanning the scene and speaking aloud.

"This is Sergeant Detective Emmett Rogers. I am at the scene of a homicide, at Quirks, one forty five Maple Street. A woman lays sprawled out across the floor. The woman's arms are positioned underneath her, as if to break her fall.

The back of her head and her long blonde hair are streaked in rusty-brown blood, as well as her clothing below the hair. Blood pools across the floor spiralling out in two long streams. Footprints are noticeable, as if someone stepped through the drying blood. The weapon appears to be a pair of scissors, found beneath the victim. I have marked both of these."

The man spoke aloud as he walked around, carefully avoiding contaminating the evidence, by stepping over a paper cup.

"A coffee cup... possibly one of those lattes is overturned. I'm sure the forensics team can determine this if necessary. Its contents are also spilled on the floor and countertop. Coffee is spilled at the front door and possibly on the shoes. The second victim's shoes are not on the bruised victim, but on the floor. The shoes can be found near an overturned ladder, at the front door. It appears the woman, who appears unconscious, may have been carrying a ladder and toy stock to place on the shelves, when she slipped in the blood.

The man paused to think.

"This might be a setup by the second victim to cover the actual crime. The woman, however, seems to have the victim's blood all over her clothes and hands like she crawled through the blood. I believe there are two possible scenarios here. One the owner of the shop, one Amelia Kelly (the unconscious person), murdered her employee or unknown victim and set this up to appear a perpetrator broke in and killed her accidentally hurting herself in the process. Or two... it is at it now seems that she stumbled on the crime scene and harmed herself."

He pulled out a notebook again and examined the room taking some more taking notes.

"Is it a robbery gone wrong? It is too soon to tell. The store owner will be en-route to hospital as soon as the EMTs have arrived. Interview to follow. The time is now ten twenty a.m.," he concluded turning off his recorder.
He examined the room scribbling on his notepad.

~0~

Now
Lily and Detective Emmett Rogers

T he man's eyes turn and his vision focused completely.

A woman entered the store. His eyes took in her tall and slender form and her long shimmering brown hair, pulled into a tight roll. He noted she was closely followed by the Emergency technicians and gave a sigh of relief. The woman entering the store had brilliant blue eyes. He had a feeling she often turned heads, even dressed as she was, in her business attire. But he noted something about the way she walked screamed money and upper class.

"Oh no, Amelia!" she screamed and tried to rush to Amelia, but was stopped by the man's arm.

"This is a crime scene ma'am. We don't want you disrupting our evidence. Let the EMTs and detectives do their job. Then you can go to ...you're er...friend?" Sergeant Detective Rogers commanded.

"Crime scene? What has happened?" Lily asked politely, wanting to be cooperative.

"Ma'am, I'll know better after I assess the scene. Until then, please remain near the front door." ordered Detective Rogers briskly.

"I promise I'll stay out of the way; but at least can I get her Adrienne Changs?"

"What or who, are Adrienne Changs?" said Detective Rogers looking totally perplexed.

"Shoes, those shoes right there!" Lily pointed to a pair of heels lying behind the yellow tape.

"You're worried about shoes? Woman! Do you have any idea of what's going on here?" Detective Rogers snapped, shaking his head.

"You sexist pig!" countered Lily under her breath.

"Men!" Losing her temper now and louder she continued, "Those shoes are worth five hundred dollars! And she probably wore them for what a half an hour? And you want me to walk away and leave them to be destroyed in some kind of liquid!"

"Liquid that's blood! And five hundred dollars for shoes? Is she crazy?" Detective Rogers asked dumfounded.

"No! She's not crazy. How dare you?" Lily asked suddenly outraged.

He was smug wasn't he? Handsome yes, but oh so smug, she questioned herself. That wasn't important. Amelia was injured on the floor and he questioned her? Instead of letting her go to her cousin! What was wrong with Lily? Why was she so worried and focused on the shoes? They were only shoes. Amelia was injured; who cared about footwear?

"Sorry, ma'am, the shoes are evidence now. Name? Occupation? Address?" Detective Rogers barked, ignoring her statement.

"I want to see your identification first, and then you'll get the information," insisted Lily.

"I am Sergeant Detective Emmett Rogers," the man revealed, showing his police badge.

"Oh that's funny," Lily uttered laughing, "If you and Amelia were introduced it would be Aem and Em."

Lily followed this up by hysterically laughing and then alternatively crying. What was wrong with her? She never lost it like this. She always appeared a professional. She had seen crime scenes. She could handle this. Couldn't she? Amelia would be okay. Wouldn't she?!

"Get a hold of yourself Lily. You have embarrassed yourself," Lily heard this voice in her head, she recognized as her father's. Odd how her Dad's voice, came back to her now, she rarely saw him, since he lived in Prague and he only called about twice a year.

"Ma'am, what you are saying is not remotely funny. Are you all right? Put your head between your knees if you feel lightheaded. I think your friend's relatively fine. She might have a head injury and possibly a broken leg, but she'll be okay." Sergeant Detective Rogers then turned to the Emergency technicians (EMTs) to seek confirmation demanded ,"Right?"

"Should be. But head injuries can be serious," the one EMT replied.

Sergeant Detective Rogers shot him a disapproving look.

"Yes, the Sergeant Detective is right. She'll be fine. She'll be taken to the hospital for treatment," the Emergency Technician agreed, finally.

"See...what did I tell you? Now that we have that out of the way; I need to see some identification and then get some answers to my questions. Name? Address? Occupation? The reason you are here?" Detective Rogers barked at Lily.

"Amelia's my best friend and more. This should have been the greatest day of her life, her opening of her new store; a one of kind toy and collectibles retailer. A grand opening and now it's ruined. Who did this to her?" Lily asked, uncharacteristically wringing her hands and still trying to regain her calm, as thoughts of Amelia's demise threatened to enter her mind.

"Ma'am, she slipped in blood. She hit her head on the floor and on the ladder. No one harmed her. She did this to herself," explained Sergeant Detective Rogers.

"I realize she's clumsy, but she didn't put blood there to trip in," defended Lily angrily.

"No, the blood was spilled by whoever killed the woman behind the counter."

"Someone is dead behind the counter?" Lily responded shocked and surprised.

"No comment; as I explained Ma'am this is an active crime scene. Now as I asked before what is your name?" Detective Rogers insisted forcefully again.

"Lily Kelly-Brooksfield. My husband is Horace
Brooksfield, the mayor. We live down the street on
Beaconfield. Do you want the number? It's nine hundred
and sixty-two." she replied condescendingly.

"If you're Mayor Brooksfield's wife... then you're the
Crown Attorney." Coming to this realization, Sergeant
Detective Rogers hid a sigh.

"Please update me on this active crime scene, now,"
commanded Lily pulling back her shoulders.

Emmett Rogers put on his professional face and smiled.
The smile was just so warm and inviting that Lily felt warm
all over. Lily frowned back at him; she was just felt so
angry. This cop who grinned back at her was the biggest
reason. She was a married woman. She shouldn't be
attracted to a cop who apparently existed to give her grief
and solve a murder. She threw back her shoulders again. It
was okay to look at someone attractive, she excused herself.
Everyone looks, and most of the time it meant nothing. It's
only if you acted on any attraction it became wrong. She
would never act on the temptation. Besides he appeared to
be the most annoying man she'd ever met.

"Ma'am, you know I can't fill you in on any of this case.
You'll have to recuse yourself from this case, as you're
familiar with the crime scene." Detective Rogers
emphasized, once again interrupting Lily's thoughts.

"Why don't you just come out and say what you think. You
consider me a suspect," Lily uttered.

"A lot of people are suspects in my book. I have to make a case for them committing the crime or I have to eliminate them as suspects. And don't attempt to solve this yourself; amateurs just get in the way." Detective Rogers explained, his eyes wandering.

Lily was slightly amused. Detective Rogers thought she wanted to insinuate herself into this murder investigation? She might not have before that comment, but she did now. He seemed to be focusing on Amelia or Lily as his prime suspect. Lily knew neither of them had committed this murder, so that meant she had no choice but to find out for herself who had committed this crime. She would pretend she wanted nothing to do with this situation, even as far as passing it off to her underling Barbara. After all she could always investigate behind the scenes.

Spotting the emergency technicians Detective Rogers exclaimed "Oh good, the ambulance has arrived to take the victim to the hospital. Now can we can get down to brass tacks; you can fill me in on these people and anything else you know or have held back from me."

"I want to go with her," Lily protested.

Lily pulled herself back taking several steps back putting distance between herself and this cop. It was odd, how alive she felt when she jousted with him. He was a cop investigating a murder and she was married.

"Stop this now Lily!" She told herself.

"Ma'am, I realize you want to go see your friend. Before I could release you from the scene, I need something from you. We need you to identify the other victim. Maybe you'll recognize her when I turn over the body." Detective Rogers explained, softening a little, as he slipped on another pair of gloves.

"Only if you'll stop calling me Ma'am. Call me Lily or Crown Attorney Kelly, but not Ma'am. It makes me feel eighty years old."

"If it will get you to identify the victim...thank-you Crown Attorney Kelly."

"Let's look, shall we?" Lily agreed.

Lily took a breath as she gathered herself to observe who lay there dead. She gasped as she stared over the counter to see the back of the woman's head. She covered her mouth in horror.

"Good grief! I never realized they appear so alike from the back," replied Lily shocked.

"Who do you think she looks like ma'am?" demanded Detective Rogers.

"What did I say about ma'am? Don't they give you sensitivity training at Police College? You want to know who this is? This is Megan, Megan Fowler. She's an employee of Amelia's. But she works evenings she's...is....was a college student. I can't believe this is Megan. Megan is such a sweet girl and worked part-time to be able to go to school and support her mother. Why would someone kill her? Do you think it's possible someone mistook her for Amelia?" Lily rambled, tears slipping from her eyes.

"That's a possibility, ma'am. We will explore all aspects." "I know the drill, Sergeant Detective Rogers." Lily gave the detective a mock salute, "Why can't you admit that they mistook Megan for Amelia?"

"We don't have any of the facts yet, Ms. Kelly," replied Detective Rogers.

"What about Amelia? Is she in any danger?" asked Lily. "If I were to speculate, I suppose that could be a possibility," Detective Rogers answered non-committally.

They both watched as the technicians gathered the evidence and blood samples and took pictures before the body was taken away.

"Will someone be assigned to guard her and keep her safe?" Lily asked getting exasperated.

"That's in motion, Crown Attorney Kelly," Detective Rogers explained, trying not to sound annoyed that she's telling him how to do his job.

Detective Rogers and Lily turned as another cop swaggered into the store. Burly and well over six feet tall, his hair was dark like Detective Rogers. Unlike Detective Rogers, this man preened like a peacock; Lily was aware of the type. Guys like him smiled with their mouths and not their eyes. They thought all women should admire them and only them. She noted his smile went as far as his lips.

"What have you got here, Emmett?"

"Nothing you need to be concerned about, Brad," Detective Rogers replied, obvious tension showing between the two. "You should be able to get some great publicity out of this one," Brad said loudly to Detective Rogers.

Brad then strutted over to the murder scene.

"It's my case, Brad," Detective Rogers insisted.

"I'm not trying to interfere," Brad persisted walking around, "I just thought if you needed some help I would lend a hand. It doesn't look like something you could handle on your own."

"I don't need help, thanks, Brad. I don't need you messing up my crime scene." Detective Rogers declared "I've got it all under control.

"It doesn't look that way to me. I would solve this case quickly. You could use me in your corner," Brad continued. "We don't need you. Now the Crown attorney is here, so I have it all in hand. Goodbye, Brad." Detective Rogers practically spat.

"Ah, the lovely Crown attorney Kelly is here. Can't go now," Brad exclaimed trying to sound charming but failing miserably.

"And you are?" asked Lily putting her full aristocratic chill in to her voice.

"I'm Brad Owens, at your service, Attorney Kelly. Sergeant Detective Brad Owens. I use to be Emmett's partner," Brad explained smiling and pointing to Detective Rogers.

Detective Rogers rolled his eyes. "Thank God you're not anymore," He stated under his breath loud enough for only he and Lily to hear.

"So what do you think, Crown Attorney? Was it a robbery gone wrong?" asked Brad.

"I'm not sure. Why do I bother to tell you this? This isn't your case," Lily commented suddenly not willing to share with Brad.

She didn't know why. Something about his smile, and the way Emmett Rogers had reacted to him made her dislike him. Brad's smile was phony, like a used car salesman. It was slick and slimy. That wasn't fair to used car sales people. Lily was sure they were more honest than this phoney, Brad Owens. Lily had come across a lot of people in her job. She certainly felt she was a good judge of character. In fact, she could spot a phoney a mile away. Detective Emmett Rogers, unlike Brad Owens, appeared like he knew his job. She'd heard of him many times, but had never run into him on the job until today. Thank goodness for the Internet on her phone. He was a dedicated cop. He had done his time and had come up through the ranks, strictly on merit. Detective Rogers didn't seem to like Brad Owens and that was reason enough for Lily not to trust him.

Emmett Rogers had an exemplary record as a police officer; she trusted his instincts and knowledge over this smarmy, Detective Brad Owens. He'd get to the bottom of this. Lily wished he would let her leave soon and check on Amelia. They had spent their teen years together and were as close as sisters. She'd always felt responsible for Amelia, being two years older. She wanted to make sure Amelia was okay.

"Okay. Well if you don't need my help, I'm leaving because I have work to do. There are other crimes to investigate." Brad answered leaving, "See you around Emmett."

"Not if I see you first," muttered Emmett under his breath.

"So am I free to go?" Lily demanded.

Emmett then offered her his pen.

"I have your address, so as long as you sign here in my notebook. "You are free to go," he said gesturing.

Lily glanced over at Detective Owens and watched him leave before reaching for the book. She then signed her signature with a flourish. Detective Rogers scanned the signature, thinking momentarily it was just as elegant as Lily. He shook his head, reminding himself to stay connected to reality.

"So I am free to go, Detective?" Lily repeated.

"I'll be checking in on your friend, of course, and I may need to follow-up with you later, but as of now, you are free to go." he smiled, already exhausted.

"I would expect nothing else from you, Detective Rogers."

As she got into her car, Lily breathed a sigh of relief she had finally been able to leave the store. She buckled up her seatbelt and put her car in gear.

Backing the car up, Lily pulled out into the street and narrowly missed getting hit by a car, she didn't view. Luckily the other driver slammed on his brakes. She noticed the male driver shouting, "Stupid woman driver" as she read his lips in her rear view mirror. He was justified in his anger. It had been her fault, but she didn't have time to dwell.

She headed down the road toward the hospital; despite her
resolve her mind wandered. She thought about poor
Megan's mother getting the news of her daughter's death. It
would kill Lily to get news like that about her adopted
daughter, Rose. What kind of monster kills a young
woman? Why did, whomever it was, have to kill Megan? It
wasn't a robbery, she'd read in Detective Rogers' notes,
when he gave his notebook to her to sign her statement. As
Lily drove, more questions flooded into her head. Was
Amelia the real target? Megan certainly appeared like
Amelia from the back.

Amelia didn't appear too hurt. Maybe she suffered a
concussion? Concussions could be serious; she knew from
her readings. The EMT hadn't said Amelia was in serious
condition though. Not that the EMT could explain before
Emmett Rogers got on his case. Revving the engine, she
waited impatiently for the light to go green. Once Lily
reached the hospital, she could reassure herself, Amelia was
all right.

~0~

Excerpt from Stray Bullet

Preface:

In the small town of Driftwood, Colorado, under starry skies, residents went about their business. The town was now ready for the arrival of the new sheriff having gussied up the urban decay with a few coats of paint. The new sheriff would see the bad parts of town soon enough the mayor thought and turned over in his bed and went to sleep. The hospital looking after a few patients was unusually quiet under the full moon; other people in the settlement getting ready for bed and then turning on late night programs or setting alarms and climbing into bed. Across town a man getting ready for bed after a long hard day at work completed his paperwork, stripped naked and stepped into the shower. As the water ran down in torrents the shower glass doors shattered, the man fell to the floor and rivets of blood ran into the drain. He was the first to die that night.

A few doors over gunman entered killing the husband and wife in their beds and the children as they slept. Blood covered the floor and ceilings in those rooms. None of the neighbours heard a peep they simply slumbered on. Other homes across the town were entered and the residents, husband wife and children were also shot and killed. No one had time to shout out or call 911. It was all over in a few minutes with no time for whimpers only the muzzle of silencers doing their jobs and hitman scurrying into the night.

"It's done, boss. The teams are leaving the state. Yes, I'll do that now. He's coming in the morning. I'll check in after I meet him. His name? All I got is G. Bullet not sure of his first name, it's not on any paperwork. . See you, tomorrow… okay Friday," the man said into his prepaid cell phone and then took out sim card breaking it into pieces. Then he discarded it in a nearby bin at the now decrepit old pulp and paper mill. He had to go to work soon. A new sheriff was coming to town and he wanted to be there to greet him.

~0~

Chapter 1 – Friendship Trumps Bullet

My name is G and I'm on my way to a new life to become a sheriff in a town called Driftwood. Sounds boring, doesn't it. If you'd asked me five year ago I would have told you of course it was; but now this is what I need and my daughter needs…a nice quiet life, in a quiet town, where I could raise my daughter without whispers and rumors. You want to more about that statement? I'll get back to that, but I'm told people will want to know about me a subject I'm not really comfortable talking about.

Asked to describe myself I would say I'm tall over six feet…okay six feet five inches. I am muscular as I lift weights. I'm not overly muscular just enough to take down the bad guys. Some people think I look like Tom Selleck in his youth, personally I don't see the resemblance.
G. is a short form for my first name but I don't like to talk about my real first name. Let's just say my parents grew up in the happy-go-lucky seventies and were heavily influenced by the weird names that people gave their children. What you still won't give up? You demand that I tell you my first name? You want to play the guessing game?

My first name is unmentionable I don't talk about it ever!!
My last name is wait for it...Bullet...I know a clichéd name
if you ever heard one. Honestly, it's my name. It has been
mine my whole life.

My last name had raised a few eyebrows can you imagine
how many chuckles I've gotten when I tell anyone my full
name? Still can't guess? Some of you have deducted
correctly. So now you know why I usually don't divulge
my first name.

In order for you to understand the relevance of my last
name I'll have to explain more about my family and their
origins.

My grandfather when escaping persecution in Russia came
through at Ellis Island and decided to Anglicizing his name
to Bullet; so my dad used that and now I do. What's that
you like to know grandpa's original name? Well so would I,
unfortunately he took that name to his grave leaving no
clues behind. But he was great man, a hard working cop. I
come from a long line of cops. With a last name like Bullet
it tends to earn respect being a cop.

Grandpa was killed on the job by some backward gangsters
bent on destroying one another. My dad swore he never be
a cop and went to San Francisco were he promptly fell in
love with my mother went to the police academy there and
then impregnated my mother.

After I turned one he decided he needed family and got a job as a cop in the city where his father had served and brothers now served as cops. When he worked there for six months he had planned to send for mom and me and marry her. Unfortunately the first day on the job he ran into a domestic situation and was killed in the line of duty. He hadn't told his family about my mother or me so we came as a surprise when mother showed up with me in tow for the funeral.

When I was four years old, my mother learned she was dying of breast cancer. My dad's three brothers, James, Bennie, and Alfred also cops, stepped up to raise me. They were a demanding bunch always pushing me to be strong and tough. I had to be resilient and learn all the fighting techniques that they taught. Let's say I am proficient in a number of fighting techniques.

Their younger sister, my Aunt Louisa was a teacher and just starting her career when they took me in however Aunt Louise found time for me. She made my childhood more normal though my uncles would often say she shouldn't coddle me. My uncles drove her away with their constant beratement and by the time I was in my teens she moved to teach in Colorado to save her sanity. She still managed to chide the uncles into letting me visit her in Denver in the summer for two months; the best two months of the year for me.

Getting back to my uncles they hated my first name as much as I did (though I think they liked me even less; but did their duty). They also felt that I had come out of nowhere so they nicknamed me Stray and it stuck; that's what most of the cops on the force called me. Aunt Louise was the only one who ever called me; by my first name.

Aunt Louise had recently retired to a small town called Driftwood Colorado and I wished she had been closer especially when I had run into the wall of blue at my job. Cut to today as I told you earlier I'd taken a new job as the sheriff in Driftwood Colorado.

As I drove to the Sheriff station; I saw that the downtown area was newly painted but other parts were decrepit and rundown. Stores had been closed and signs had been posted that said for rent but the places looked like they hadn't been rented in a long time. The back alleys showed signs, of hookers working their wares with discarded condoms.

The town was surrounded by trees; but the main source of jobs in the past had been lumber and the company had pulled up stakes and moved away. Factories and brickyards were closed. Some of the homes have seen better days and the downtown core was eerily quiet, with vacant storefronts lining the streets. Crime which in the past hadn't been a problem was suddenly up and maybe that's why the Sheriff had quit? But that was the reason I was here. I'd shape this town into a town we could all be proud of again if the re-elected mayor could do as he promised and bring in the jobs. I wanted to be happy here.

I'd just dropped off my three year old daughter with my Aunt Louise. Stella Marie, my daughter seemed okay with the new place and Aunt Louise; but was I? Aunt Louise was sixty years old and a retired school teacher. Why was I so worried? First day jitters obviously. Aunt Louise had my back. She knew what idiots her brothers really were and how they valued their friendships even more than family. Being a single father I needed her more than ever.

Aunt Louise had urged me to apply for the vacant job of Sheriff after hearing about my troubles as a cop in a suburb of Halton, Illinois. I don't want to get into those troubles right now. Today was a new day and I decided it was going to be great even if it killed me. Just kidding! I was not going to get killed like my dad had on the first day of the job. Nerves were getting to me.

Sure it was hard settling into a new place for a child. A little voice worried that I had made a mistake; but this was a new start for both of us we should be happy. A month ago I had been offered my dream job, Sheriff of a small municipality in Driftwood, Colorado. Driftwood looked to me like a small town of three hundred people where I'd be happy raising Stella-Marie.

 The streets were tree-lined; the cookie cutter houses had beautiful floral displays out front. The lawns were immaculate green and lush. Children rode their bikes up and down the streets with no fear of predators or gunplay. The people had seemed friendly and warm when I came for my interview for the job. What more could we want? I'd thought.

I'd done my research; but nothing had prepared me for the men all walking out on me. I stepped into the Sheriff's car. This blue flu wouldn't do! I knew from the dispatcher that the other cops were not happy with my appointment; but damn it was my first day on the job and they had a duty to serve and protect the citizens of Driftwood.

How could the four deputies just not show up for the day?
Calls to their residences had gone to voice mail so they
were even avoiding talking to me. I had to put my foot
down hard or the men would never respect my leadership.
I'd already faced a wall of blue in my old job; people
pulling out the old politics line and drawing in ranks on the
thin blue line. I'd wanted a new start to change the
harassment I'd faced in my not so fair city over the last
three years.

A bit of a long story which we'll get into later, but suffice
to say the line in blue was put up against me; simply
because I stood up to another cop who committed a crime.

Driving down the road to go to my new deputy's home I
grew angry. Hadn't I been through enough of this crap from
the guys in Halton? I had been harassed day and night by
those assholes.

I had to pull myself together; anger would not solve this
problem. I could show them I was in charge but
approachable. I was an outsider, hired on line. Hell I hadn't
even met any of this guys but I would get along with them
they just had to give me a chance. No that sound desperate
and I wouldn't be that anxious. I would be the best Sheriff
and boss they ever had.

I parked the squad car and mounted the wooden steps on the house. I knocked lightly on Deputy Gregory Barnes door. No answer. I gave it my best thundering police knock and the door swung open of its own accord. I pulled my service revolver and entered the residence wily. A smell of dead berries and apples entered my nostrils. I felt in my pocket and swished my menthol medicated lip balm under my nose. My adrenaline kicked in and suddenly I felt exhilarated and hyper aware.

I followed the putrid odor to a bedroom and found the late Greg Barnes with two bullet wounds to the heart surrounded by a dried rusty brown pool of blood. He'd been there at least two days. Nothing was disturbed in the home. No overturned furniture, nothing seemed out of place. He lived alone; so no help there. Was it a rogue girlfriend? Why was he dead?

What the hell? The first day on the job and my deputy is murdered? I needed those other cops that hadn't come to work today to help me solve this murder. Damn them and their blue flu.

I made the call to the coroner who was on call for autopsies. Then I secured the scene and called in the neighboring counties police force on loan until I could find my police force.

Less than an hour later, I had two officers, Alfred Jones and Paulo Scarlatti, I sent to the two of them to retrieve the first officer Joseph Paciocco on my list. Imagine my surprise when he called back to tell me that my other officer, Joseph Paciocco was dead too. Two shots to the heart and it looked like the same felon. Was I going to find all my missing officers dead?

A quick search of the other residences found all of the bachelor cops dead shot the same way. The family men with their families at home were dead too; but so were all their family members. They had all been shot with one shot to the head in their beds. They had not stood a chance. This was a professional job as each scene had been carefully scanned and nothing was left to find in the way of evidence other than the blood and bullets.

All in all the dead were Gregory Barnes, Joseph Paciocco, Jack Abrahams, Paul Jones, Harold Jones and his wife Cheryl, their two children Gail, and Fred, Vincent Vecchio and his wife Paula Antrim (both cops on the force), their baby, Adrian a newborn was alive in his crib and was taken into custody of the Children's Aid until a relative could be reached. Also dead were Robert Di Salvio and his wife Rebecca and their fifteen year old son William and their daughter Helen eight years old, Kas Mahmoud his wife Dayita, and their three sons, Aaban, Aahil, and Aatif ages five seven and nine.

What in the hell was going on? Someone had killed whole families. Why? Did they know something someone didn't want them to know? Was it retaliation?

This meant looking into backgrounds and finding out things people didn't want you to know. Being sheriff didn't make for a popularity contest in any case but this would have to be handled very delicately.

The police officers on loan couldn't continue to investigate this; I only had a temporary loan of their services for today. Even if I wanted to investigate I had to have help. I needed to call the FBI pronto and I knew just the guy my former partner Gordon Chum.

I dialed Gordon's number by heart. He answered on the first ring asking me about the new job and then said he'd speak to his boss and get the okay to bring a team down as soon as possible.

Meanwhile I was trying to comfort the staff left at station and ducking calls from reporters from all over the country and residents of Driftwood who were demanding to know what had happened. I took deep soothing breaths…Gordon would be here soon we'd get to the bottom of this. Penny Ambercrombie the office dogsbody and police dispatcher took charge and hustled the troops off to their stations to work on the tasks I'd given them.

Penny was tall and lean possibly one hundred and ten pounds though it was hard to tell for her clothes hung on her in non-descript browns that did nothing to enhance her looks and she was well over five feet eleven. Her hair was a rich chestnut and was wound tightly at the nap of her neck into a bun. Her eyes were her most striking feature that not even her terrible clothes sense could hide as they were a glittering emerald green that showed immense interest and intelligence. She appeared to be in her late twenties though her skin was leathered with the weathering an outdoors enthusiast had.

I could see that Penny was an asset to me and the sheriff's station in my job. But first I needed to call Aunt Louise and Stella- Marie and hope my daughter wouldn't get too upset that daddy would not see her until tomorrow at the earliest.

I picked up the phone and called the number by heart. There was no answer. Where could she be I wondered? My question was answered in the next few seconds by my office door swinging open. There my Aunt Louise stood with Stella Marie. Aunt Louise demanded, "Gunnar is it true? Are they all dead?"

The next thing that happened was three year old Stella-Marie jumping in my arms and saying "Daddy, I missed you."

I closed my office door no sense in putting on a show to the remaining troops and I hoped no one had heard my aunt utter my first name. Stella-Marie took the chair nearest me.

"I want an answer Gunnar."

"Not in front of the c.h.i.l.d."

"Ch.. i… ld, child, that's me," my precocious daughter answered.

"Stella-Marie already knows all about this. She turned on the television while I was in the bathroom and she heard about all your deputies and their families being found dead. She insisted I bring her here."

"Then you both know what I know. I'm investigating and I've called in the FBI."

"Daddy, are you safe? In that movie with the Kung Fu guy they tried to kill him and then killed his family," Stella-Marie answered.

"What have you been watching?"

"I remember his name. I love Jean Claude van Damme movies," Stella-Marie stated.

"Me too, pumpkin and we're safe. I haven't been here long enough to be mixed up in whatever is going on here," I reassured.

"You'll find the bad guys?"

"Daddy will find them. That's what daddy used to do before he had you," I answered.

"Be careful," Stella-Marie said with adult wisdom beyond her years.

"Stella-Marie is correct. You need to stay safe."

"I promise both of you, I will stay safe."

"We'll trust you."

"Can we have dinner together, daddy?"

"Of course we can my apple dumpling."

"I'm not an apple dumpling."

"No you're my little pumpkin."

"You're silly, daddy."

"What would you like for dinner? Pizza? Chinese food?"
"Pizza! I want pizza!!"Stella-Marie chimed.

I ordered her favourite Hawaiian pizza and we forgot work
for a few minutes as we ate. Stella-Marie told me about her
day between bites. Stella-Marie sounded happy and
adjusting well to living in this new place. She didn't seem
too worried about my job anymore. She kissed me goodbye
and said, "Get'em, daddy. See you tomorrow, nighty,
night."

I breathed a sigh of relief my daughter seemed happy
despite all that was happening. I was the new sheriff so the
danger to me from who ever committed these murders must
be minimal if any, so my family was safe. Still I told Aunt
Louise to keep Stella-Marie indoors and keep the doors
locked reporting any suspicious activity to me.

Gordon arrived a few minutes later, "I'm Special Agent
Gordon Chum FBI," he said showing his badge then
continuing he said, "I'm here to take over this case."
"No. You're not you're here to assist me and the good
people of Driftwood."
"I am here to serve the people yes and if that means taking
over the investigation in a town that has seen fit to kill all
its police officers save one..."
"How dare you? This town is peaceable. There is a
perpetrator or perpetrators who have committed a heinous
crime but we will get to the bottom of this."
"You should have recused yourself Sheriff."

I heard Penny Ambercrombie gasp and then mutter under
her breath, "What a maniacal idiot and a kook to boot."

"No, you shouldn't! This was my first day on the job. I was to begin tomorrow but I thought I'd get in and do a little paperwork first. I am imminently qualified to investigate this. I hadn't even met these men or their families; but I care very much about what has happened to them. They are police officers and my squad. Every one of them is mine so this crime was done against me and my family. Do you understand?"

"I understand the feeling and I promise not to step on your toes, Sheriff. My men and I are at your disposal in this investigation. You are in charge. Perhaps we could discuss the particulars before my colleagues get here?" Gordon stated.

"Please follow me this way to my office, Special Agent Chum," I answered.

"Call me Gordon," my pal offered.

"People call me Stray, or Gee," I stated.

Gordon pretended to be shocked and lifted an eyebrow at me. Penny looked at Gordon with disgust but went back to the front desk of the station.

Gordon entered my office and shut the door, loudly. Spotting the pizza he said, "That went well."

"Yes, it did. Did you see the dispatcher, Penny Abercrombie craning her head and her ears to listen to you?"

"I saw her when I came into the station. She was frowning at you and giving you dirty looks when you weren't looking like she didn't believe you belonged here."

"I noticed those looks all day," I answered.

"That should be the end of that you can thank me now. She is directing those looks to me now and I'll wager she'll spread all over town how you defended the honor of the dead."

"Thanks Gordon for the assist; but how will we can we keep up the lie?"

"We begin a new friendship," Gordon said calmly then continued, "I hope you saved me a few slices of that I'm starved and my team is checking into the No-Tell Motel down the street within the hour."

I smiled and nodded handing him a couple of slices. It was good to see my old partner again.

"You are staying with me and Aunt Louise aren't you?" I asked.

"Lucky for you or is it me they are limited space in this town to stay and of course this allows me to begin a new friendship with you. All my agents have taken up the last rooms in the motel so I'm grateful your aunt will put me up. You did ask her didn't you?"

"Didn't think I had to, you know Aunt Louise loves you." Gordon raised another eyebrow.

"Fine I'll call her now."

I dialed and Aunt Louise answered her cell phone on the first ring. Aunt Louise said of course Gordon was staying here. I told her not to tell anyone we knew her and she agreed after I told her why. Then she said she had to go as she had pulled over to answer the cell phone.

"So it's settled?" Gordon asked.

I nodded.

"What a terrible first day on the job for you pal," Gordon commented, "Especially after what happened to you more than three and half years ago."

I thought back to what I had been through the last three and half years and I found myself reliving that chaotic time in my mind.

I'd been about eight years on the job in the city of Halton, Illinois, a cop, just like my dad and grandfather and uncles before me. The city had gone to the gangs. . It was two steps and one step forward. Every time we turned around; another shooting another victim of a drive-by. Just the other day the victim was a seven year old kid innocently riding their bike! Luckily the kid lived; but we actively hunted for the shooter or shooters. I should have took that as an omen seeing as my grandfather and my dad lost their lives in the police service, but I went merrily on my way doing my job not expecting my life to come crumbling all around me.

A routine call to a richer neighborhood for a disturbance started it all. The dispatcher didn't think to tell me it was a domestic disturbance and the man had a gun. I'm always careful in those situations; more careful then the average cop but if you don't know you can't take precautions.

I knocked on the door and announced myself and shots barreled through the front door grazing my forehead and tearing my knee apart. I burst through the door grabbed the shooter and he shot me again. That should have got me accolades and medals right? After all I was shot doing my job, but no, all of those rightly went to my partner, Gordon Chum. The third shot resulted in a thigh wound that almost made me bleed out on the spot if it wasn't for the quick work of my partner Gordon Chum securing the prisoner and belting my thigh. Okay, so I got a medal or two, but Gordon was the real hero. See why he was the first man I called when my force had been gunned down.

Gordon is a second generation Asian American. A good looking fellow and kinder than most men, he speaks softly and carries a big stick. People underestimating him rather walk away unscathed. Gordon standing at five foot six weighed roughly two hundred and ten pounds of pure muscle. He knew every fight technique I knew and more. He saved my life a time or two.

Gordon was arguably one of the best partners I've ever had. Gordon saved my life after I was shot on duty and secured the scene until back-up could get there. He also called for an ambulance for me. I was carted off to a hospital where I spent the next three weeks in intensive car being prayed over by my fellow cops, and the rest of the city.

Whatever chits they called in with the big guy upstairs it worked, I survived and I should have been happy about that; but all I could think was I missed my moment I was supposed to die like my dad and my grandfather before me on the job. It wasn't that I was that different when I came out of the coma. Okay, so I had a few scars inside and out. My forehead now sported a scar that I could cover with bangs and temporarily bum leg. The leg didn't seem to want heal in fact at one point they threatened to take off my leg; but good old Gordon helped me fight them on that and the knee healed to the point I could walk on it. But it wasn't good enough for work, at least not then.

Suffering from self-loathing (and yes a little post-traumatic stress disorder, if I truly admit it); I began to be curt with everyone closing myself off from everyone and everything. My wife, Gina took the brunt of all of this. I was cruel to her at every turn. When she came to visit I'd ignore her.

I knew I needed help from the police shrink but I couldn't accept or admit that I, the wonder boy actually had a problem. Gordon begged me to quit loathing myself so much and making everyone else around me miserable but I didn't listen. I was content to wallow in my anger and self-loathing.

Weeks went by and Gina seemed unhappy despite her forced saccharine with me. She gave me an ultimatum get help; or she would leave me. I decided I wanted Gina so I found a shrink of my own choosing Doctor Collins for his add in the Yellow Pages.

Doctor Collins turned out to be a woman.

Don't get me wrong she wasn't a fantasy (that blonde fantasy with legs up to here and hiding behind glasses); no she was more like your grandmother. Non-descript, her silver hair short and curled tight to her head. Her voice was soft and she always offered me milk and cookies before a session. I kind of felt weird at first like she was family and I'd never been all that chatty with family anyway. I had so much trouble talking at first that I'd just sit there and stare at the walls; but after a few sessions she got me to open up about my childhood and then finally about the shooting. I began to feel better and worked on getting my knee back in shape so I could return to work.

I had a routine and I followed it. Therapy followed by afternoon sessions of psychotherapy. With the drugs Doctor Collins prescribed and all our talks I began to almost feel normal again. Okay, so I'm lying; I still had a few stray thoughts that I was a failure and that I should have died; but I labored hard to overcome them and worked on being nicer to my ball and chain. I even began to buy her flowers. As for my leg it was almost good enough to return to work.

Doctor Collins had scheduled my appointment for two p.m. on a Friday and I had looked forward to getting it over with and going home to surprise Gina. A cop buddy had offered me his family cottage and I planned a trip to the Poconos for the next week. I'd already called Gina's work and got her the next week off. It would be a fantastic surprise for her and a chance for us to just lay back and enjoy our weekend. I could even cook all the meals that I caught from the lake as it was loaded with fish.

I decided to change my appointment and let Gina know that it would now be at noon instead of two p.m... Surely I could charm my shrink into seeing me earlier and if not well then I see her next week after my trip. I arrived at the doctor's office to find a note on the door. It seemed my shrink. Doctor Teresa Collins had died suddenly this morning and they were rescheduling. A number to call followed the announcement.

Died! And all they thought about was their schedule? Devastating and only then realizing how close I had gotten with my shrink I fell to the floor crying and took about a half- an -hour to recover enough just to pull myself together. I told myself over and over everything would be okay but I didn't really believe it.

Enough of this shit!! A little therapy and I turned into a wimp; who cried at the drop of a hat. I was a Bullet and we were strong manly types; made of steel not mush!! People died!! Get over yourself I admonished myself. I had a life... a wife who loved me despite myself. It was time to man up and be the husband she deserved. I just had to get away with Gina. I'd go home and surprise her now.

Stopping at the gas station to fill-up and walking into pay I spotted roses. I picked some up and thought how pleased Gina would be. She deserved this after all I'd put her through the last two months. She'd surprised me two weeks ago, telling me that she was pregnant. I was overjoyed looking forward to our baby coming in six months. We had a new beginning and I would make her as happy as Gina had made me.

I thought about the look on her face; her joy at our baby and decided to book her favourite restaurant before we left town. We could then leave at nine p.m. I'd drive all night and we reach there by morning. It could be done despite my gimpy leg. Okay so I lied, I wasn't fully recovered; but soon I would be. My physical therapist was pleased and said I might even be able to go back to work in a month.

I went home opening the front door with my key and... You know what happened? It was that other old cliché...husband comes home and finds his wife naked doing the tango with another naked man.

I didn't recognize him from the back as he jumped out the window, naked clothes in hand. She could tell me who he was in her own good time. And I had plenty of time as I seethed and wanted to kill him but not her. I didn't want to hurt her at all I just wanted to take her in my arms and make this go away.

I took huge breaths and then realized it takes two to tango. I had brought this on with neglect and coolness towards her when all she did was support and love me. I took deep breaths to calm myself and rationalized. I was sure this was just a one-time thing.

I'd heard women could get quite horny in pregnancy I obviously had let her down.

I had been a terrible husband moody brooding, distant and angry. Gina deserved better and I could forgive her this. Couldn't I? Sure I was angry, but I would never harm Gina despite my thinking for her lapse in judgement. I had stared at her five foot nine naked figure with its well-endowed breasts and tiny waist and wondered how she hid our baby in it.

Her curly black hair fell in ringlets to her waist. I realized I loved her. I loved our baby. It had been my neglect that had driven her to this; I was prepared to forgive her and take her on my planned trip. We'd been married fifteen glorious years, okay so not glorious, fiery but she was also pregnant and I wanted my child to have a stable home with two parents one of them me. I'd been spared so my kid could grow up with a dad it was as simple as that.

I told Gina all of this and she laughed. It seems that she and her paramour had been carrying on since day one of one of our marriage. Once more she had an amniocentesis last week and received the results this morning the baby was his not mine. I was devastated all those dreams of playing catch with my daughter. Taking her to daughter and daddy dances. Having her look up to me, with hero worship came crashing down. Yes, I know it could have been a boy; but I had my heart set on a girl.

I admit it I went against all my principles and begged her to
stay and claim the baby was mine. We were married so the
baby was legally mine. She laughed that twinkly laugh that
I knew so well and I had to restrain myself from retaliating
as she told me she already left me I just hadn't noticed.
Gina said she was tired of living a lie. Now that I knew it
was all out in the open and she file for divorce and move in
with him. She lunged at me slapping me and asked why
could I be like him?

I want to hit back at her but I couldn't if I it back I wouldn't
be any better than the men I arrested who abused their
wives.

Why couldn't I be like him? The man that she slept with,
she raged. I was stupefied and getting angrier by the
moment I knew I needed to leave before I regretted losing
my temper; but I needed to know who had replaced me.

She laughed again and said I find out soon. I begged her to
tell me and she did.

HIM? I fell to my knees. How could it be him? No, it
wasn't Gordon Chum; but someone else I considered a
friend and brother. Gordon wouldn't do that to me. The
dirty dog who had betrayed me had been a partner, a mentor
and good grief the man was old...fifty-five if he was a day
and close to retirement.

Why had she cheated on me with my former partner Derek? He'd broken the cop code you didn't sleep with another cop's wife. He'd slept around I heard how many women he'd been with had she? I told her and she laughed telling me it was his cover story. She continued snickering and said at least every woman didn't try to pick him up in front of her. She packed her bags and then trounced out the front door to join him at his house.

I thought I could handle it all and maybe I could have if she hadn't come back a half an hour later saying she'd changed her mind. She stripped to her skivvies and begged me to change her mind. What's a hot blooded male to do? I wanted to prove I was the better man, the better lover, so I turned my back and began stripping too.

That's the last thing I remember before waking up in hospital. How I got there and what happened after that I couldn't recall until much later.

The doctor kept speaking to me but it sounded like gibberish. My brain didn't want to understand. I don't know why. I closed my eyes, but before I drift under I hear them talking.

"Will he be okay now, doctor?" Gina asked.
"We'll know better when he answers my questions," I perceive the doctor say far away.

I heard footsteps as someone left.

A voice I recognize as Gina whispered in my ear, "You stupid son of a bitch. Why didn't you die? You'll wish you had now."

I struggle to wake before she can harm me but it's like moving under quicksand. I hear an alarm sound and footsteps run into the room.

"What did you do you now, you evil bitch?" I heard Gordon yell as I feel myself falling through layers of unconsciousness into nothingness.

~0~

Please look for this book June 2017

Excerpt from Dreams Can Kill

Chapter 1- Survival

The rain pelted down on me, as I struggled to come to my senses. My head felt like it had split in two, as if little lumberjacks had taken up residence. I opened one eye. The world spun sideways like a ride at the fair. I tried shutting one eye, then the other. I nearly fell back to sleep. I opened my eyes again, fighting the sleep which wanted to overtake me. I shuttered my eyes again, as my stomach protested. My whole body manipulated, bruised, bent and broken like some old rag doll discarded.

Sleep...sleep would solve my problems, my brain protested. No! I had a reason I needed to stay awake and alert...A little sleep, a part of me protested again. No, I must stay conscious. But I remained so tired. I dragged myself across the pebbled ground. My right leg stuck out at an impossible angle, obviously broken. I saw by lifting my head slightly and turning it that there appeared to be a road up ahead. I had to get to the road. If I dragged myself that far, surely I would be rescued?

But it was oh so hard, to drag yourself backwards, when you couldn't perceive where you were going. Oh no, what if he came back. He would finish me off...finish what he had started.

He who? Who was this person, who left me to die? Why couldn't I remember? Don't panic... the thing to do is right now is to reach help; then and only then would I be safe. I caressed large pieces of gravel which cut into the back of my head. I sensed I was close to the road. I reached out with my good hand and touched a paved surface. I knew I didn't have much strength left. I experienced the energy drain quickly leaving my body. I tried to fight the drain, but the world faded to black.

~0~

Chapter 2- Time Flies When You're Having Fun

I opened my eyes slowly. A tube appeared to have been inserted in my arm, feeding me intravenously, another tube down my throat as well. The lumberjacks in my head had been replaced by a dull achy sensation, as if I wasn't quite there. I suffered from weakness all over, but my body didn't have the same sensation, as when I had blacked out on the road.

My leg felt whole again and yet my leg didn't appear to be in a cast, or slung up on a tripod. How much time had passed? This definitely looked like a hospital room. The walls were pale white and I lay in a single bed. I rested in a private room how about that?

A nurse in a white cap entered the room. She grabbed my wrist and she proceeded to take my pulse. Alarmed, she stared straight into my face, "Well! Look who is awake. Welcome back to the real world," she proclaimed.

I tried to speak and realized the tube in my throat prevented that. Why was a tube in my throat I wondered? How long I been here? I assumed I looked scared because the nurse explained in a soft voice, "There, there honey, you take deep breaths, easy now."

"Why don't I go get the doctor? He can come and have a look at you and remove the tube from your throat."

I tried to nod my head in agreement but my head moved like lead. It seemed like eons before a man in a white doctor's coat appeared at my bedside. He appeared tall and lanky; with dark curly brown hair and warm deep blue eyes. Without any preamble he announced, "We will now remove this tube. Take a big breath now."

The tube came out as I gagged. Now I could ask the questions which plagued me.

"How did I get here? And where am I?" I tried to ask, croaking out the words, as if my voice hadn't been used in a while.
"Speak slowly. Here, have sips of water," answered the doctor.
"How did I get here?" I repeated, sure that I had been speaking clearer because I had taken a sip of water.
"I don't know who found you, but an ambulance brought you here in critical condition. You had a broken leg, some broken ribs, and a fractured skull."
"I came here in critical condition? So I've been here awhile?" I asked shocked.
"Yes, you've been here awhile. You were at a different hospital first. You are in Andrews' clinic now."
"Your condition appeared to be perilous there for some time. They lost you twice. We had placed you in a coma to let your brain swelling go away. Then we didn't know if you would ever come out of the coma."

He continued to explain like he couldn't quite find the words. But why would a doctor have trouble explaining a medical condition?

"I guess time flies when you have fun," I stated flippantly, hiding fear I didn't quite understand and becoming puzzled.

Why did he say first they then we? Hadn't he been there?

"I would like to examine you to see how you're doing now and get an update on your condition."

"I'm good. As you can see," I answered in response.

"I don't know if you even realize, but your speech isn't as clear as you think. You're slurring your words," he stated.

"I'm sure the words will come easier in time, but I'd like to check your reaction time and some other physical reactions."

What could he be talking about? I wasn't slurring my words. Was I?

The doctor began his examination. A flashlight flashed deep into my eyes. I blinked in response, as the light, so bright, made my eyes hurt. His response seemed to be to write down something on the chart, and pick up my wrist to take my pulse and blood pressure. He then listened to my chest with his stethoscope.

I moved my head and tried to sit up, but the effort zapped all my remaining strength. I surprised myself at how I felt like a newborn baby. He continued his examination. I grew tired but fought the sensation. If I closed my eyes for a moment, would the feeling would go away? I closed my eyelids and fell fast asleep.

I ran over hills. The night appeared so dark, and ink black; I could barely view two feet in front of me. My feet stumbled, as I tried to see the uneven ground in front of me. My palms clenched with sweat, as my heart pounded like the organ would jump out of my chest. I turned around, my eyes darting from side to side searching for my pursuer. No sign, but I knew he wasn't far behind.

My hair in a high ponytail, whipped at my face, as I picked up the pace in my flight. He seemed close enough, that I had the sensation of his breath on my neck... so close he might reach out and touch me. I turned again to see if I could glimpse him near, and I saw a man. But what puzzled me was what materialized in the man's face. Where his face should be, a gaping black hole yawned.

How could this be? The thought plagued me only for moment, as fear gripped me and survival instinct kicked in. Realizing if he caught me I would be killed, I ran stumbling over rock and uneven ground. When the inevitable happened, I tripped falling to my knees. He had me. There was no escape from my fate. I would die now. I struggled as he grabbed my left wrist twisting my arm.

This appeared no dream, I might awake from; he had me now and he would kill me.

I twisted slightly trying to free my wrist but he grabbed my other wrist and shook me slightly saying..., "Quite a dream you were having, but a dream none the less. Nothing can harm you now."

I stared into his face and slowly his look changed, from the faceless man, to another face entirely. This wasn't the man in my visions; the demon in my nightmare. I knew in my heart this remained an altogether different kind of man.

This face with smiling blue eyes radiated warmth, and kindness. His face stayed gentle, not violent. I had been dreaming and had mistaken his touch for the man in my dreams. I flushed with embarrassment.

"You are quite awake now? I won't harm you. Now, do remember me?"

I stared at him, slowly waking up, and realizing where I was.

"I'm your Doctor, Doctor Andrews, at your service, my lady. We met before when you awoke from your coma," he continued speaking softly, and gently, bowing at the waist and smiling.

Shouldn't I have recognized him immediately? Heat rushed to my cheeks, as I turned red in embarrassment.

I was a fish out of water. I didn't like the way I reacted; like something had happened and all was a secret to me. I liked to be in charge of my life every aspect, and right now it seemed like I appeared in charge of nothing.

"How long have I been here?" I whispered, trying to speak louder.
"I would have said it's a lot longer, than you think," he replied cryptically.
"Do you always answer a question with a question? I want an answer for my query," I demanded angrily.
"What do you remember?"
"I believe I asked you to stop making this an interrogation. If you must know, I remember waking up a little while ago the nurse came in and then you came a little later," I answered exasperated, wondering what could be wrong with me. I didn't get angry so easily. Did I? Why did I behave this way? Everything he said seemed to make me angry.

"Your little while ago was two days ago...," he explained, breaking off as if afraid to say more.
"But that's impossible..."
"You fell into a restorative sleep. It is not uncommon for patients who have been in a coma to do so."

"Two days? I slept for two days?" I commented incredulously.

"Yes," Doctor. Andrews stated.

"How long was I in a coma?" I asked worried to hear what he might say.

"What month do you remember?"

"You have to be in charge, don't you? Questions! Questions!" I replied, delaying the answer. I was suddenly afraid that I'd been in this coma far longer than I realized, and grew angrier.

"I know you're scared. Are you sure you want to know? The information can wait," he insisted.

"I'm not scared," I lied with false bravado, "I remember quite clearly the month is March."

"It is the eleventh of September nineteen hundred and seventy-one. Do you remember what happened the day of the accident?" he asked.

"That's not possible. I can't have been in a coma for six months. Why do you lie to me?" I spat at him.

"I know it's hard to assimilate but time has passed and it is September," he insisted softly, but firmly.

"Why do you persist in a lie? What do you have to gain with this preposterous story?" I demanded; still not ready to believe this.

"Exactly what do I have to gain? Sharron, I'm not lying to you," he stated sadly.

Until that moment I hadn't given any thought to my name, but as Doctor Andrews called me Sharron, I realized I wasn't even sure if that was my name. I didn't have a clue what my name was. My name might be Sharron, but I didn't recall the name. My name could be Mary, or Angela, or any other name in the world. If I had a surname, I couldn't remember it either. A huge blank spot stood where any recollection should be.

How could my last memory be of March, but I still had no recollection of my name, er names? This was normal after a long coma. I decided.

Perhaps my memory had been so underused, and only had temporary gaps? Or I was hungry? Yes, it had to be one of those things. A temporary aberration of the mind... No need for me to worry. No, need to share any such information.

My memory was only hiatus. That had to be the answer. Give it a few days and my memory would all come back. There was no need to tell the doctor, especially since my recollections would all come back. Absolutely not, I reasoned.

After all what good would it do to tell him? He'd look at me either with sympathy, or call in a shrink. I wanted none of the sympathy, and whispered glances which would follow. So I had a few memory gaps, nothing to worry about. It was perfectly normal after a coma, I reassured myself.

"What will you do with all this information Sharron?" asked Doctor Andrews suddenly concerned.
"I must admit the information was a bit of a shock to find the month was September and not March, but I'm over the surprise. "I'm hungry what does it take to get food around here?'' I demanded, quickly changing the subject. Besides I was ravenous.
"I think you can start some light foods, some soft foods, Jell-O soup etc.," Doctor Andrews spouted. Turning to the nurse he commanded, "Nurse get a light meal for my patient."
"Certainly Doctor," the nurse replied, coming into the room rather quickly, at his summons.

Just when I thought I had successfully gotten rid of the doctor, he turned around and said... "I know you are rather tired and hungry right now, but I'm sure you to want to discuss these revelations later today."

How could I get him to change his track? I didn't want to discuss my memory loss with anyone. I wasn't ready for anyone to find out I didn't know who I was. If I told him, would he treat me like a mental patient?

No, I wasn't going to tell him, or anyone. I needed to fake what I remembered. They'd never know, I couldn't remember. I would then have the time to accept this myself, and hopefully everything would come back. No one would ever have to know.

Wait a minute, did he know, I didn't remember? He talked about the fact I'd been in a coma, but had he given me any knowing glances? I gave him a sideways glance. Deciding he didn't have a clue about my memory problem. I plotted to keep it that way.

"There is not a lot to talk about; but if you want to we can discuss my medical condition we can get to that later," I replied, hoping he would take my response as an agreement and leave.

Luckily for me he took the hint. Maybe he would even forget to come back and discuss this later? No, I hoped for too much, but he did look convinced that I'd talk to him later. Good then he'd go away.

"I will return later, Sharron."

He then left taking his questions with him. I breathed a sigh of relief. Now alone with my thoughts, surely I'd conjure up a memory or two. First I would eat and refuel. That would help the memories, as well as my stomach.

I stared at the food the nurse had brought in. I'm starving to death and the nurse gave me not enough food to feed a rabbit? I tried to pick up the spoon and found my hand wouldn't cooperate.

"Would you like some help?" the nurse asked kindly.
"I can do it myself," I responded stubbornly.

Although I had found it difficult to raise my hand to my mouth, that soon became easier. I found by clamping my hand around the spoon I could manage to feed myself. It was then I realized how much work I had ahead of me. The nurse watched, so I smiled at her like everything was fine. She smiled back and left.

I soon made short work of the food and wanted to move on to the therapy I recognized I needed. I would set the memories, or lack of them aside, and working on building up the muscle tone and abilities I'd lost. When the body restored itself, I would begin to remember. I understood without being told, that I had to begin like a baby to exercise my limbs and I wanted to start immediately. Let's be honest. I realized I could remember something. I grasped now that I was an impatient person, at least when it came to doing things I had to be doing. I called the nurse on the call bell to ask about therapy and exercises.

"Yes?" I heard a disembodied voice somewhere over my head say. Momentarily puzzled, I then realized the voice came from an intercom.
"Sorry to bother you but when can I start therapy? I need to get my limbs moving," I explained.

"Dear, you are barely out of coma. I'm sure your doctor would want you to build up your energy first. Or wait at least until you started solid foods."

She sounded surprised and had a hint of censor in her voice. No support there. I wanted those six months back, but clearly that wasn't going to happen. Move on, I told myself. I'd wasted six months sleeping, time to fight back and get back into fighting form as they said. But who had said that?

I somehow knew I was a fighter. I'd have to do everything myself; something I knew I always did. But how did I know that?

I thought about what would work, and what limbs need to work. My hands needed to a work out. Okay, they need to grip. How do you make hands stronger?

You give them something to grip. Squeezing something soft, medium soft, would work. Where to get something to work my grasp? I couldn't even get out of bed. My limbs were useless, absolutely useless. My hand shook in weakness, from forcing the stupid thing, to do its job and feed me.

All of this began to feel hopeless. ..No, I wasn't some stupid helpless female. I had to figure out a plan. You're on your own, I told myself, nothing new. You can overcome any odds. Think, Sharron, think!

How about some finger exercises? Slowly working each finger, and then in tandem, I would get back movement. I began the exercise I devised. It sounded so simple when I had thought of how to exercise the hand, but painful and tiring. Work through the pain, I told myself. Isn't that what you've always heard?

I forced myself to do the exercises for what seemed like hours, until I couldn't take the pain any more. Then I decided to exercise my arms. Gripping well enough to pull myself up to the bar over my bed, I reached I'm with my right hand to grab the pole. My fingers won't cooperate. My fingers are weakened and my grip slipped. Damn it! Even simple exercise was impossible.

"Nothing is impossible," a voice spoke loudly in my head. But whose voice did I hear? My memory had fled, if it was ever there. I only comprehended the voice had been someone I loved, and respected. Was this a father, or a father figure? I knew I was bone weary, and a great sea of lethargy stole over me. It would be counterproductive not to take a nap, I reasoned. Surely a short nap would restore my energy and I would begin again.
I closed my eyes soon I began dreaming. At first the dream appeared happy. I viewed myself in a beautiful home and grinning at someone I couldn't see.

I smiled and felt great joy, but the sky grew dark and I found myself outside on a field. The moon overhead slowly covered by clouds, and I grew terrified. Something was wrong. The faceless man chased me once more. I ran over rocks and streams and more rocks. He kept coming and coming. I knew he'd soon be on me. He nearly had me when I willed myself to wake up saying... This is a dream and I want to wake up now.

I awoke gasping for air like I had been running a marathon. A strange man sat by my bed. His hair appeared dark, practically black, greasy, and slicked back. He had black thick glasses that he peered over like they were a prop.

An oversized suit coat in plaid and matching pants completed the picture. Despite his harmless appearance, he struck terror to my heart. What gave me the idea he put on this persona, like a piece of new clothing? I think it was his face which seemed to give it all away, like he tried too hard to portray someone he wasn't.

As I gazed at him, he jumped from the chair he sat and exclaimed…"About damn time you woke up out of the coma Sharron. I thought you laze there forever."
He then continued, as if choosing his words carefully, "Oh Sharron, this is the most wonderful day of my life." Then he pulled me to him, fiercely.
"Let go of me, this instance. Who do you think you are? I said don't touch me! And quit acting and looking around there's no audience for your play," I blurted out, before I stop myself.
"Sharron that's not funny. Quit joking. You always had a wicked sense of humour, but I'm not laughing." the man stated, sounding annoyed and grabbing my wrist.
"I said let me go, and I meant every word. Now kindly take your hands off me," I demanded at the top of my lungs, struggling unsuccessfully to free myself of the grip, he now had on my wrist.

Taken back by my yelling, he let me go, but he still continued to treat me, like a bug under a microscope. Suddenly switching gears, his face changed. It was if a curtain went down over his face. He took on a concerned look and then a hurt look. I admit he nearly had me fooled.

I started thinking I had forgotten a boyfriend, but surely I wouldn't suffer from such bad taste.
He wasn't my type. He seemed quite violent too. I wouldn't have been so foolish to get mixed up with a weirdo like him! Would I?

"Sharron quit staring at me that way you're making me uncomfortable. I'm not amused here...Wait a minute you're not kidding .You don't recognize me at all. You don't recognize your fiancé?"

I recognized somehow that he was put on an act. No, I wasn't engaged to him. If I had been it would boggle my mind. He had to be lying, I decided. Why I didn't know, but I knew he lied.

I had no sparks with him. In fact something about him gave me the creeps. He repulsed me and made my stomach hurt. He certainly didn't sound sincere. He put on an act ... but why? He grabbed my wrists again, once again in a vice grip. I struggled valiantly, but his grip tightened and I couldn't handle his fierce clutch in my weakened stated.

"Let me go you, caveman. I don't know you and what is more, I don't ever want to know you," screamed at him fighting frantically.
"Sharron you cut me to the quick. Why do you say such things to me?" he whined, letting go of my wrist, but gripping my arms even tighter.

Maybe it was because of my dream, but suddenly I was terrified. Why did they leave me all alone with this crazy man? Where was everyone else? Couldn't they hear me shouting?

"Let me go. Let me go....Don't touch me," I yelled at the top of my lungs, and then screamed, hysterically "Help me someone help me."

As I started to pull harder frantically to be free he stilled held fast. What kind of evil demon had me in his grasp? I tried to bite him, but that was impossible; finally in the answer to my screams were footsteps running. Seconds later a nurse and Doctor Andrews entered.

"Let my patient go immediately. I said let her go," Doctor Andrews growled, pulling the man's arms behind his back. I breathed a sigh of relief. I was safe. Doctor Andrews had saved me.

"I wasn't hurting her! What kind of a man do you think I am? Gee, I have more bruises than her. She acted crazy, so I grabbed both her arms to calm her," the man explained, sounding plausible.

Surely Doctor Andrews and the nurse who followed him in, didn't believe his act?

"Your technique doesn't seem to have calmed her, but it certainly frightened her," Doctor Andrews said, checking my blood pressure and heart rate.
"You can't tell me what to do. She's my fiancée I can speak to her anyway I want," complained the man, loudly.
"You've upset my patient. Her blood pressure and heart rate is elevated as well. This is not good for my patient, so I can tell you what to do. What is your name?" demanded Doctor Andrews.

"Titus Brown is my name and Sharron is my fiancée," the man replied a little too quickly.

Doctor Andrews consulted his clipboard. He pointed to it and then announced, "This is the approved register and you're not on the list. Leave now, Mr. Brown, or I'll have security escort you out of the facility."
"I'm not going anywhere. Who do you think you are?"

Mr. Brown showed his true colours, I thought. They would trounce him faster than you could say Jack Robinson.

"Mr. Brown, so far I've been pleasant. The nurse has already called for a security guard. I suggest you leave now and don't come back, or you will find yourself with a trespassing charge and jail time," Doctor Andrews said through his teeth.
"I'll be back with my lawyer and you'll be sorry," Mr. Brown menaced.

Two security guards entered and forcefully removed Mr. Brown from my room. I began to shake like a leaf. I tried to stop, but I grew frightened. Someone had tried to kill me and that is why I was in the hospital. What if it was Him, Mr. Brown?

They wouldn't let him take me when he talked to his lawyer? Would they? Words I hadn't want to share, spilled out of my mouth, first in torments, and then at a screeching level.

"I don't know who the heck he is, but I do know I don't know him. I'm not his fiancée. Don't let him come back lawyer, or no lawyer. I don't want to see him. Someone did this to me! I wouldn't be surprised if the person was him!" I guess I appeared a little too hysterically and forcefully, because the next thing that occurred was Doctor Andrews plunged a needle into me.
"Please, please don't. It's not necessary, really. I'll be good," I pleaded too late.
"It's a little sedative. I don't like your colour, your blood pressure, or your heart rate. You've had a nasty scare and your body isn't able to cope with this right now. Calm down now," he said comforting "Go to sleep."
"I think I hate you," I replied vehemently.

"That's okay, you can hate me if you need to," he answered, smiling.

Damn him and his handsome smile! Something about the grin, made me want to smile back and tell him all my secrets.

"Don't leave me alone. He might come back," I pleaded as I drifted into a deep drugged sleep.

~0~

Please find any of these books from the excerpts on sale at Amazon in e-book or paperback. If you enjoyed *A Stitch in Time* please consider leaving me a few words at your favourite retailer and if you liked the excerpts and would like to read more of my books please check out one of my other books listed on the next page at Amazon.

Sincerely S. G. Lee.

~0~

Books by S. G. Lee

Murder Mysteries

Love's Labour's Won
A Tiger's Heart Wrapped in a Player's Hide
Reborn – a novella~ prequel
A Penny Saved A Murder Earned
A Diller A Dollar A Really Dead Scholar
Betty Blue Lost Her Holiday Shoe
What Will Poor Robin Do?
The Kelly Murder Mysteries-Book 1-3
A Stitch in Time
Stray Bullet
Dreams Can Kill

Short Story Books
Murder Most Fowl
Jack be Nimble
Day of the Dead
Legends, Folktales and other Stories
The Stuff of Nightmares
ObsessionX2

Christmas
Christmas is Calling
The Christmas Card
The Christmas Angel
Visions of Sugarplums

Poetry
A Poetic Touch - The Human Condition

~0~

www.ingramcontent.com/pod-product-compliance
Lightning Source LLC
Chambersburg PA
CBHW061203170626
46809CB00003B/1227